Wells, Tobias
   A die in the country. Published for the
Crime Club by Doubleday, 1972.
   188p. 4.95

Title.

A DIE IN THE COUNTRY

by Tobias Wells

A DIE IN THE COUNTRY

THE FOO DOG

WHAT TO DO UNTIL THE UNDERTAKER COMES

DINKY DIED

THE YOUNG CAN DIE PROTESTING

DIE QUICKLY, DEAR MOTHER

MURDER MOST FOULED UP

DEAD BY THE LIGHT OF THE MOON

WHAT SHOULD YOU KNOW OF DYING?

A MATTER OF LOVE AND DEATH

Tobias Wells

A DIE IN THE COUNTRY

Published for the Crime Club by
Doubleday & Company, Inc.
Garden City, New York
1972

All of the characters in this book
are fictitious, and any resemblance
to actual persons, living or dead,
is purely coincidental.

ISBN: 0-385-01669-7
Library of Congress Catalog Card Number 72–79429
Copyright © 1972 by Doubleday & Company, Inc.
All Rights Reserved
Printed in the United States of America
First Edition

To our very fine neighbors on Howe Street,
not a one of whom appears in this book.
Except, perhaps, for Theron.

A DIE IN THE COUNTRY

The real estate saleswoman looked bemused. "To tell you the truth," she said, "there aren't too many houses in Wellesley in your price range."

My hackles rose. I have sensitive hackles. Brenda said quickly, "But surely you have something to show us . . . ?"

The real estate saleswoman looked thoughtful. "I wonder if the Pinkham house has sold. We didn't list it, it was an exclusive with another broker, but"—she smiled and reached for the telephone—"it won't hurt to ask."

Brenda and I looked at each other while the saleswoman exchanged pleasantries with, apparently, a friendly rival. Our baby was due in three months and we'd decided that our wharf apartment in Boston, while a thing of joy to us, was not the perfect spot for child-raising. A house was the thing, with a yard and grass and trees—only, where?

Until recently, I wouldn't have had as much choice. The statute required a police officer to reside in the city or town of his employment. But in the last year the law

Copy 1

had been changed and now we could live anywhere within reasonable distance. North Shore, South Shore, west of Boston, even the Cape if I didn't mind commuting on the traffic-bound Southeast Expressway.

We chose Wellesley, some 15 miles west. Or maybe I chose it, I'd been to the town before on business and it had impressed me. An affluent community, noted for its schools. Baby boy or baby girl Severson, we hadn't been able to agree on names as yet, would someday go to school. So here we were, sitting across the desk from Mrs. Maynard of Maynard Realty, watching her hang up the phone and hearing her say happily, "It's still on the market and she'll meet us there in fifteen minutes."

"What sort of house is it?" Brenda wanted to know, not, I thought, unreasonably.

"It's really quite a good buy. They've done a great deal of work on it lately, a new porch and all. It has an interesting yard and an excellent view. It's up high, you see, and you can see the entire college from the third-floor window." The college she referred to, I assumed, was Wellesley College.

"Three floors?" asked Brenda.

"Yes, it's unusual in that respect, too, at least in the suburbs. It's Victorian in architecture but modified through modernization. It has, let's see"—she referred to a card—"four bedrooms, the third-floor one is almost a studio bedroom, and three full baths. Modernized kitchen, two-car garage, fireplace, a very nice porch as I mentioned, and even a brick patio."

"How much is it?" I asked.

Mrs. Maynard beamed. "You're in luck. The price has

been reduced." She named it. "The owner was trans-
ferred and had to move out of town so he's willing to sac-
rifice."

"How long has it been for sale?" I asked suspiciously.
It sounded like a lot of house for the money.

She looked vague. "I'm not sure. Several weeks, I
guess. As I told you, we didn't list it." She reached suddenly for her handbag, stood up. "Are you ready? My
car's just outside."

"We might as well look at it," Brenda told me.

I shrugged. Some choice. One house. In our price range,
as Mrs. Maynard had said, making it sound as though all
we could afford was peanuts. If Wellesley were too rich
for our blood, we could go elsewhere. But not farther
out, commuting distance from Wellesley wasn't bad, a
couple of miles into Newton or Weston and I'd be on the
Mass. Turnpike, twenty minutes from Division One.
Well, how about Newton or Weston? Only, Newton was
a city and there were good parts and not so good parts
and no doubt what we wanted would be just as expensive. As for Weston, it was zoned for an acre or so and
anything with that much land cost money.

We got into Mrs. Maynard's Cadillac and she took off.
Down the main street, past the police station (I knew a
fellow there, Dennehy was his name), into the shopping
center, fine-looking shops, expensive I'd bet, and over a
bridge.

"Here we are," said Mrs. Maynard turning left, "right
in front of you, at the top of the hill."

It was a tall white house with a peaked roof, the kind
of house that little children draw, an oblong sort of box

shape on end with a pointed roof. There was a big window in the front with small panes and a cement and cinder block porch around two sides, with a wrought-iron railing.

The shutters were dark green and there was a post lantern at the end of the driveway. Lots of trees around and a tremendous bush of some sort in the front corner, rhododendron, I thought. I'd never seen one that big. The house looked freshly painted, in pretty good shape.

"Oh," said Brenda.

"What's wrong with it?" I asked warily.

Mrs. Maynard laughed merrily and wheeled into the drive. "Frances will be along any minute," she said when she'd turned the motor off. "Want to look around the grounds?"

I was looking at the house next door, or trying to look would be more like it. It was pretty well hidden under trees and behind bushes, high bushes, low bushes, tall grass. It appeared to be gray, but from where I stood it hadn't been painted in some time. "Who lives there?" I asked and found myself talking to thin air. Brenda and Mrs. Maynard had disappeared.

I walked around to the back of the house and found them standing on a brick patio looking up. The house sat on the brow of the hill, the land rose gently behind it, and was topped with a rock that appeared to grow from the ground like a mountain top. Behind the rock was a level lot with a stone wall to end it. In front of the rock was a rock garden and a stone retaining wall.

"How interesting," Brenda was saying.

"It would be the devil to mow," I commented. "I'd have to lug the mower up those steppingstone steps."

"And to your left," said Mrs. Maynard ignoring me, "is a little patch of real woods."

"How lovely," said Brenda. "So private."

"There you are, Mildred!" The second lady realtor had a good deal of very blond hair piled on top of her head and wore a bright professional smile.

"This is Mr. and Mrs. Severson, Frances." Mrs. Maynard stepped modestly back, protocol, I presumed, when the realtor "listing the house" appeared.

Frances—I hadn't heard her last name—flourished keys. "You're really in luck," she told us, "this is an extremely livable house and the price has just been reduced. So few in this price range, you know, and I really feel this is a great deal of house for the money."

"That's what I told them," beamed Mrs. Maynard.

We walked around to the front, stood beneath two coach lanterns that flanked the door which Frances opened, and went in. The floor of the hall was carpeted in blue, wall-to-wall, and so was the living room off to the left and the room behind that which held a fireplace and had mahogany-paneled wainscoting. Shutter doors, white, separated the two.

"This was the dining room originally," Frances explained, indicating the wainscoted room, "but the family who owns it found it too large for a dining room, really a waste of good space, so they made it into a second living room or family room and used an expandable table when entertaining."

"What a good idea," said Brenda.

"They sure liked blue," I muttered. I could make out places where pictures had hung on the pale blue wallpaper. It would need repapering, I was thinking, and the woodwork would need repainting.

There was a pantry, the old-fashioned kind, and the kitchen was done in red and olive with natural pine cupboards and a wooden ceiling. "Cypress," said Frances. "Quite effective, don't you think?"

"Oh, yes," Brenda agreed.

Looking at the patterned walls, I thought, more wallpapering.

The stairs had white rails and a mahogany baluster, they went up maybe eight steps and turned, repeated the process, rather like an angular winding staircase. More blue carpeting, all the way up three floors.

I had to admit the bathrooms were all right, even though there was no john on the first floor. "They've all been done over," Frances told us. And three of the bedrooms had been newly papered, not my choice of colors, but they would do, I supposed.

The view from the third floor was as advertised. I could see a good part of Wellesley College, handsome brick buildings and rolling hills, quite nice. But it was such a big house for two, about-to-be three people. And so much to do to it . . . I didn't want any part of it. I stood there staring out while the women talked behind me. There was a house across the street, an odd sort of thin white house with fresh paint. "Who lives there?" I asked, pointing.

"Oh, that's where Rudolph Wharton lives," Frances said it as though I should certainly know Rudolph Wharton. "It's an old neighborhood, but a very respectable one."

"And who may I ask is Rudolph Wharton?"

Mrs. Maynard smiled. "You'll have to forgive us. He's a selectman and naturally we think everyone knows his name."

"What's in here?" Brenda's voice came from the third-floor bathroom.

Frances went in to join her. "That's a cedar closet. Very handy."

"Oh, yes."

"When did you say this place was built?" I asked Mrs. Maynard.

"Around the turn of the century. But a good deal of work has been done, new plumbing, wiring, and so forth. And the taxes are quite low."

"I haven't seen the cellar," I reminded her.

"Yes, that will round out the tour." And we trooped down blue-carpeted stairs to the kitchen, made our way down into the old cellar. The floor was cement and the walls made of massive boulders, whitewashed. "The washer and dryer were down here," Frances told Brenda, "but personally I'd like it upstairs. It could be done."

I thought, more expense.

I made up my mind then and there that I definitely didn't want this house. If this was all Wellesley had to offer, we'd just look elsewhere.

One week later we signed the purchase and sales agreement and one month later we moved in.

Our tomcat sat in the middle of the blue carpet and

looked disdainful. "You'll get used to it, Mein," I told him. "You'll have to."

"There's a lovely patch of woods out there for you to roam in." Brenda opened the side door for him to look out. He studied the terrain, moved cautiously out onto the porch, sat, studied again.

"Oh, Knute, I'm just going to love it. I felt it was right the very first minute I saw it. I'm so happy you said we could buy it!" And Brenda threw her arms around me. She had to bring them from a long way off, she was in her seventh month and what counted was up front.

"I should have taken a course in home repair," I told her. Handy man, I was not. I'd lived in apartments so long, never had to do anything more difficult than change a light bulb.

"Don't worry, darling. We'll take our time. And it will be fun, making it really ours."

There was a flash of gray fur from the porch and one tomcat went flying after one squirrel. They disappeared into the woods, the squirrel making furious noises.

"Good heavens," said Brenda, "do you suppose he knows what a squirrel is?"

"Only the Boston variety," I answered. "These fat suburban squirrels are something new to Mein."

"I hope he doesn't catch him," she said.

"Who? Mein or the squirrel? Come on, I brought a case of cold beer to share with the moving men. Let's break out a bottle and sit on our front stoop until they get here."

"Oh, Knute." She looked shocked. "What would the neighbors think?"

"They'd think we were sitting on our front porch having a beer waiting for the moving van. What else would they think?"

"Out back would be better, darling." She put her arm in mine. "We want to make a good first impression."

I looked down at her dark head. She was turning into a suburban wife right in front of my eyes. Who would have thought it of the independent city girl who'd been the right hand of one of the fastest lawyers in the East before I married her?

"All right," I acquiesced. "Out back." And I took two beers out of the trunk of the car, opened them and we drank out of the cans, sitting on the edge of a brick flower box that had some little green things sprouting up out of it. "What's that?" I pointed to one. It looked like a baby tree.

"It's an oak." Brenda looked wise. No doubt remembered from her New Hampshire youth. "Pull it up, you'll see the acorn. Can't have an oak tree in the middle of a flower box."

I reached down and pulled out the miniature tree and looked up to see a huge, strange woman staring at us from the driveway. Her hand was extended and in it was a broad leather leash. At the end of the leash was a dog that fitted her perfectly. It was a Saint Bernard. Its tongue was hanging out, it was pulling in our direction and as our eyes met, it began to bay.

"Hello," I said, starting to stand.

"Don't get up." Her voice didn't belong to her at all, it was soft, slightly southern in accent, and young, like a teen-ager's. Teen-ager she was not, I guessed her age to be maybe fifty. She had a headful of wheat-colored hair that sprang out from her big head in all directions, very curly, a woolly nimbus. She wore dark glasses so I couldn't see her eyes. I wondered for a second if she were blind and the dog was her guide. But no, or she wouldn't have said don't get up.

"I'm Mercy Bird," she told us. "You must be my new neighbors."

Brenda got awkwardly up. "Yes, we're the Seversons. I'm Brenda and this is Knute. How do you do." The dog lunged at her, tongue lolling.

Mercy Bird gave a powerful yank and the immense furry creature backed off. "His name is Algernon. He's very affectionate, but doesn't realize how big he is. He might knock you down in a nice way and I don't think that should happen to you at this time. Did I see you bring a cat?"

"Yes, his name is Mein Hair, my husband thought that was very funny when he named him. We just call him Mein. It got a little tiresome, explaining all the time." She gave me an oblique glance. She hadn't forgotten that I'd suggested, just kidding of course, that we name the baby, be he a boy, Eric the Red Severson. What I really wanted to call him was Leif.

"Algernon likes cats," Mercy Bird told us, "but cats don't like Algernon. I just wanted to tell you that he won't hurt your cat. Is there anything I can do for you? When is your furniture coming?"

I looked at my watch. "Any time now. We'd ask you to sit down, but as you can see we haven't anything to sit on yet."

"That's all right. I'll bake you a cake and come again.

Without Algernon. Welcome to Wellesley." She yanked, Algernon moved, she turned and they were gone, Algernon, mind completely changed, pulling her in the opposite direction. An ocean liner towing a battleship.

"She must live in that gray house hidden in the jungle," I thought out loud.

"Uhmmm—is that the moving van, Knute?"

I looked around the corner to the end of the drive. "Right—just backing in."

"Thank heavens."

She came toward me and I asked, "Are you feeling okay?"

Brenda patted my arm. "Of course. But I'm going to be pretty tired tonight, I think."

And just as the moving men got out of the van, Mein emerged from the little patch of woods with something in his mouth. Proudly he dropped it at Brenda's feet. It was what had been the squirrel.

She looked startled, her mouth opened, and she covered it with her hand. "Get it away," my pregnant wife gasped. "I think I'm going to be sick."

It took me longer than I'd expected to drive home to Wellesley after work. I found myself smack in the middle of outgoing commuter traffic at 6 P.M. and while the Mass. Pike moved well, the arteries onto and off the Pike were slow going.

Which was why I was on the irritated side when I swung into my new driveway and braked immediately. A strange car was parked in the middle of it. Who the devil, I thought, banged my car door, and marched into the house.

"Knute . . . we're in the kitchen," called Brenda as soon as I entered the hall and picked my way through a pile of boxes.

I took off my raincoat and hung it up in the hall closet. "Who's we?" I asked, heading for the kitchen.

"This is Mrs. Parsons." Brenda and a middle-aged woman with bright red hair sat across the table from each other, looked up at me.

Mrs. Parsons had a coffee cup in her hand which she put down and offered the hand for shaking. "I'm the

Town Greeter," she told me, showing a good many small teeth in her smile. "I've brought you all sorts of goodies, little gifts from the shops. And I've been telling your wife all about Wellesley." She closed her mouth and looked smug. "I'm sure you know you've moved to a splendid community."

"We hope so." I was dying for a beer, but remembering what Brenda had said about first impressions, I thought I'd better wait. "How'd it go today?" I asked my wife. I'd felt some guilt in leaving her with a houseful of boxes, so much to do. If we had dinner early, I could get at the books, get them in the bookshelves. If only Mrs. Parsons would go.

Brenda smiled wanly. "I haven't stopped a minute until Mrs. Parsons came. I even forgot lunch, but it all seems so overwhelming . . . I told Mrs. Parsons to excuse the kitchen, it's a mess but still it's the neatest room in the house right now." She looked around. "And you can see it leaves a lot to be desired."

Brenda was right. Pans were stacked on the counters, a box of dishes by the sink, and dozens of canned foods in tins sat on the floor by a cupboard. I wondered how we'd acquired so much in so little time. We hadn't been married quite a year.

"Oh, I don't even notice," caroled Mrs. Parsons. "I'm quite used to it, calling on newcomers as I do. You'll have a lovely house when you get straightened around. You know, of course, that Katharine Lee Bates once lived here. And that Monseigneur Davis died in the bedroom upstairs."

I frowned. "Who is Katharine Lee Bates?"

Brenda echoed her, "Died?"

Mrs. Parsons' laugh was merry. "Katharine Lee Bates wrote 'America, the Beautiful.' And don't worry, Monseigneur Davis died of perfectly natural causes. He was eighty-eight." She pushed her chair back. "Well, I must run along. It's been very nice to meet you, I'm sure."

"My pleasure," I said politely and stepped aside. Brenda accompanied her to the door and I went to the refrigerator. Bless Brenda's little heart, there was beer.

"My goodness." Brenda returned, looked around hopelessly. "I don't even know where to begin."

"I'll put the canned goods away," I volunteered.

"You'd better change your clothes first. The floor's dirty."

"Okay." I took a swig from my beer can. "Where's the cat?"

"Out. He seems enchanted by those woods. I hope he doesn't bring me any more presents."

"Cats are hunters. It's their nature." I started for the stairs.

Brenda murmured something I didn't hear. I stopped, asked, "What?"

"Predators," she repeated.

"He can't help it," I told her. "And he'd never had much of a chance before to do his thing."

"Of course he can help it," Brenda sounded sharp. "That's like saying that a killer has to kill."

"They're two different things entirely," I said firmly and went upstairs.

Over a dinner of canned soup and toasted cheese sand-

wiches, Brenda said, "That Mrs. Parsons, she was pleasant, but what an awful gossip."

Through a bite of sandwich, I asked, "Oh? What did
she gossip about?"

"All the neighbors. Miss Bird, next door. According to
Mrs. Parsons, she's weird. She's a writer, it seems, only
nobody knows what she writes. And no one ever gets
into her house."

"Mrs. Parsons maybe should learn to mind her own
business."

"And that man across the street, the selectman?"

I nodded, spooned soup. "Wharton, I think his name
is."

"Rudolph Wharton. Well, Mrs. Parsons says there's a
terrible scandal going around—it seems his wife has left
him, or that's what he says, but nobody knows where she
went or when . . ."

I raised my eyebrows. "My, my. The classic body buried in the cellar?"

"She didn't say that, but she implied something like it."
We looked at each other and Brenda giggled.

"Tell me more," I urged. "This is fascinating. Just like a
true-life novel."

"Now you take the family across the street, next to Mr.
Wharton." Brenda went into a Parsons act. "Mr. and Mrs.
Arlen Farley are the parents of two teen-agers. The boy
is a college dropout, long hair and a beard, shiftless, you
know. And the high school girl runs around with a very
fast crowd. The morals of young people today—it certainly was different when I was a girl!"

"I'll bet it was, Mrs. Parsons . . ." I was about to go on

with the game when the doorbell rang. "Now who could that be? Mrs. Parsons for a second installment?"

It could be, and was, Mercy Bird. She wore a heavy topcoat with rope toggles, pile-lined boots, and a cap with earlaps. Considering it was spring and the weather wasn't cold, she looked odd. In her hands she carried a huge chocolate cake. "Here," she said, thrusting it at me.

"Won't you come in?" I took the cake and stepped back from the door. A car was pulling into the driveway across the street, a jazzy-looking white sports car, a Jaguar.

"Fink," said Mercy and I was startled until I realized the word was not addressed to me, but to the tall, dark-haired man getting out of the Jaguar.

"Mr. Wharton?" I asked.

"Thinks he's God Almighty," she replied almost absent-mindedly, and came inside. If I wasn't mistaken, she smelled of Saint Bernard.

"Miss Bird," Brenda spoke from the kitchen doorway. "Do come in. Oh, a cake. How nice."

"It's good," said Mercy Bird. "My sainted mother's recipe. One of the few things I can cook worth a damn, chocolate cake. I got the knack. Call me Mercy."

"We can ask you to sit down now," I told her, "but it will have to be the kitchen. How about something to drink? We've got coffee. And beer."

She plopped herself on the bench in the kitchen, lifted the earlaps but didn't unbutton the coat. "Have you got any buttermilk?"

"No," said Brenda, "I'm afraid not."

Mercy shrugged. "Think nothing of it. Nobody ever

has. I think Mother and I are the only people who ever drink it. I'll take the beer and thanks."

I had a sudden mental picture of Mother. "Does she live with you?" I asked, opening a beer and searching for a glass.

"Who?"

"Your mother?"

"In a way. We have talks every day. I buried her in the cemetery in the next town, even though her home was in Maine. Too far to go, down Maine. Didn't want to be that far away from her."

"Oh, I'm sorry," said Brenda.

Mercy reached for the glass of beer, took a long draught. "That's all right. We get along better now than when she was up and around, to tell you the truth. When are you going to have the baby?"

Brenda blinked. "In June. The end of June, it's supposed to be."

"Got a good doctor? That's the secret, you know. None of those quacks. Get a good doctor." She drank more beer.

"Oh, yes. A very good Boston gynecologist. Dr. Abraham. He's quite well known."

"Never heard of him. But then, I wouldn't. Never had any need for a gynecologist." She laughed. A girlish laugh, trilling up and down.

I took a can of beer for myself and sat down. "I understand you're a writer. What do you write?" If she could be blunt, so could I.

She gave me a sideways look. She had unexpected long eyelashes. "Murders."

"Murders? You mean, mystery stories?"

Mercy nodded. "Understand you're a cop."

"Detective First Grade, Boston Police," I told her.

"Can I ask you questions when I need to?"

I was amused. "Sure. If I know, I'll tell you."

"Thanks." She raised the glass, swallowed the remainder of the beer, stood up.

"Won't you have another?" asked Brenda.

"No, thanks. Got to go and take Algernon for his nightly run. Thanks for the beer. Take care of yourself, Mrs. Severson. What's your name, Brenda? I'll call you that if you don't mind. Don't stand much on ceremony."

"Of course. Do call me Brenda."

"And I'm Knute."

She nodded, started for the door.

We trailed after her.

"Come again," said Brenda.

"Thanks for the cake," I told her.

"I'll be back for the plate." Mercy Bird, without looking back, opened the door and went out.

Brenda and I looked at each other.

"That," I said, "is a rare bird."

Brenda laughed. "But, you know, I kind of like her."

So did I. Maybe life in the suburbs wasn't going to be so deadly dull after all. And when I reached retirement age, maybe I could do a book about the life and times of a Boston cop as told to . . . Mercy Bird? I wondered what name she wrote under. Next time I saw her, I'd have to ask.

I didn't get a chance to drop in on Dennehy until a couple of weeks after we'd moved. By that time, I'd done all the donkey work for Brenda and she could see to the refinements. She was set on new wall-to-wall curtains for the big picture window in the living room and she wanted them in the material that matched the new wallpaper. She'd priced them, sighed, stuck out her chin and declared she'd make them herself.

Which was what she was doing when my two days off came up and I was no help whatsoever. So on the second day I called the station, found that Dennehy went off duty at four and went down to intercept him.

The Wellesley Police Station was a neat brick building set back on a wide green lawn and hiding, or partially hiding, an equally neat, also brick, elderly housing complex.

I parked my car, went in through the front door, stopped at the desk. "What can I do for you?" asked the officer on duty. He was a husky fellow with a full head of wavy dark hair.

"Dennehy in yet?" I asked.

The desk officer checked the clock on the wall. "Any minute now."

"Okay if I wait?"

He looked me over casually. "Sure."

I took a seat on the bench in the lobby. A sergeant came in, stopped at the desk, pulled off his cap and wiped his brow. "Getting hot out," he said.

"Wait till it's summer," said the desk officer. "How did you make out with the dog?"

"Nasty brute." The sergeant sighed, put his cap back on. "Got to make out my report for the selectmen." He pronounced it see-lectmen. "That dog ought to be disposed of."

Two men in business suits came in the door. "I'll be in my office," the taller of the two told the desk.

"Yes, sir, Chief," responded the desk officer. "Afternoon, Chief," added the sergeant.

The chief nodded. He was a weather-beaten-looking, compactly built man with a hint of midriff bulge. I'd met him briefly a few years back, but he wouldn't remember and for the life of me, I couldn't think of his name.

"Who's the guy with the chief?" the sergeant asked the desk man.

"From the telephone company."

"Oh—yeah."

The front doors swung open and Dennehy came in. At least I thought it was Dennehy, his sandy hair looked about right if a little longer and the square Irish face fit, but he was older and heavier. I said tentatively, "Dennehy?"

At the same time, the desk man told him, "Hey, Dennehy, somebody here to see you."

I stood and stuck out my hand. "Severson. From Boston," I reminded him.

The blue eyes looked momentarily blank, then he recognized me. "Oh, yeah. Hey, how are you, man? It's been a long time. What brings you out to Wellesley? Official business?"

We shook hands. "I've moved out here," I said.

"Yeah? That's great. Hey, Dorsey, meet Severson from the Boston P.D. Detective Severson, isn't it?"

"That's right. First Grade now." I shook hands with Sergeant Dorsey.

"And this is Elihu." The desk man and I repeated the handshake.

"It's my day off," I explained to the trio, "and you know how it is about busmen's holidays."

"Not me." Dorsey grimaced. "I take off to the woods whenever I get a chance."

"Dorsey's our man's man, our hunting and fishing nut," Dennehy clapped me on the shoulder. "Hang around till I get through, will you? We'll grab a cup of coffee someplace, or better yet, a beer down in the Falls. What do you say?"

I shrugged. "Why not?" I sat down again while Dennehy went about his business. A couple of kids came in to register their bicycles and a pair of patrolmen reported for the second shift. The phone rang and Elihu took the squawk which appeared to be a complaint about minibikes. One of the patrolmen, looking resigned, went off to look for the minibike operators. I gathered this was a recurring problem and I thought we should have it so minor in Boston. But dull? Yes, chasing minibikes was no doubt dull. Not to say deadly dull.

Dennehy emerged, dressed in civies. "Elihu, is the chief around? I'd like him to meet my friend."

"He's shut up with the telephone company," Elihu answered and turned to pick up the ringing phone.

"Don't bother him now," I said. "Some other time."

Dennehy nodded. "I'll see you guys. Come on, Knute. I'll introduce you to our nearest and dearest beer joint. Mary's, down in the Falls."

Walking out with him, I said, "I thought Wellesley was dry."

"Oh, it is. Publicly. Except for the inn where they've got a special license. Mary's is just over the Newton line. It's quite a hangout and strictly less than fancy."

"Want to take my car?"

"Doesn't matter. Yours or mine. We can leave the other one here, pick it up later. Maybe I'd better do the chauffeuring, though. I know the short cuts."

Dennehy's car was a jazzy sports model, a TR 3 painted bright red. "Some car," I commented. "Bet you dollars to donuts you're still a bachelor."

He laughed. "You're so right. I got this baby at a police auction. Worth $4300, paid six. Not bad, eh?"

"Not bad at all."

Picking his way through traffic, Dennehy asked, "Where are you living?"

"Twenty Howe Street."

"Howe Street?" He gave me a quick look.

"Yeah. It's a short street right off Weston Road . . ."

"I know where it is. One of our selectmen lives on Howe Street."

"That's right. Wharton. Right across the street from us." I gave him an equally sharp glance. "What's the story?"

He stopped for a red light. "Somebody's got a hate on for him. Poison-pen letters."

I thought a moment. "About his wife?"

"You know about that?"

"It seems to be common gossip."

"Yeah. Well, the thing is that Mrs. Wharton took off on him. We've had a letter from her, she's out in California. But whoever writes these letters claims she's dead, that Wharton did her in. It bugs him." He moved off as the light turned green.

"But if you know she's okay . . . ?"

"Yeah, but it gets to him just the same. He figures anybody that nutty is a bad one to have as an enemy. He's a pretty good joe. Have you met him?"

I shook my head. "What does he do for a living?"

"He's a property owner. A rest home, a medical building, a block of stores, that kind of thing. I guess you could say Rudolph Wharton owns almost half of the business area of the town."

"Money, huh?"

"Must have, but he's no high liver. You've seen his house, no reflection on where you live but it isn't the Cliff Estates."

"No, which reminds me, do you ever see Kay-Kay Mason?"

He screwed his face up in concentration. "Kay-Kay Mason? Oh, yeah, the old gal on Albion Road. I think she's moved out of town. Haven't seen her in a long time." Kay-Kay, who hadn't been that "old," had been a most helpful witness in the case that had brought me out from Boston a few years back. I'd become quite fond of the lady, she'd had guts up to here. "Well, here we are," Dennehy said, interrupting my thoughts. "Like I said, nothing fancy."

Mary's was, indeed, nothing fancy. A narrow entranceway with windows painted halfway up. A half dozen men of various ages in work clothes sat in booths drinking beer. We found a booth for ourselves and ordered a couple of brews.

"Have you got any kind of a handle on this Wharton business?" I asked Dennehy.

He shook his head, nearly buried his nose in his beer. "They're postmarked Natick. That's the next town west. So whoever it is has to be in Natick at some time for some reason. They're all pasted-up words cut out of the newspapers. Mostly the *Herald* and the *Townsman*. On regular typing paper, you know, the kind you get at any dime or stationery store. With plain cheap envelopes."

"How many have there been?"

"Close to a dozen. Since January. Mrs. Wharton went away in January. There are an awful lot of nuts running loose in this world."

"You can say that again."

"Are you married yet?"

I grinned. "Very much so. My wife's going to have a baby the end of this month. You'll have to come over and meet her."

"Glad to. Can I bring my girl?"

"Why not? Thinking of taking the step?"

He shrugged. "Sometimes, yes; sometimes, no. She's a good kid. Her name is Sandi. Sandi Smith. But I kind of hate to let go of my freedom."

"I know what you mean. But you get used to it."

"That," said Dennehy, "is what my mother says. But my old man says, take your time, boy. Forever is a long, long word."

And on that, we had another beer.

"Hey, Knute, when are you going to invite us out to your new mansion?" We were having a coffee break at Division One, and Davoren, Captain Granger's clerk, was giving me what he considered to be the needle. I didn't think he—and some of the other guys for that matter— were jealous, but they had been coming in heavy with the references to Rich Wellesley.

"Any time," I said easily. "Any time after the baby's born. And that won't be long now."

"How is Brenda feeling?" This from Barry Parks, my partner, gentleman born and bred.

"Pretty good. The move was rough on her but she didn't want to wait."

Captain Granger's door opened and Davoren looked quickly around. "Yes, Captain?" he asked and Granger, looking out, said, "Knute? Can I see you a minute?"

"Yes, sir." I left my half-empty coffee cup where it was and joined him. He was about due for vacation and I thought he looked tired. It used to be once a year that he talked wistfully of retirement. Now, it was more like every six months. One day he would do it, I supposed, and it would be a whole new ballgame at Division One. I didn't like to think about it.

"Sit down, Knute. How's the new place in Wellesley?"

"Fine, Captain. We're getting surely but slowly straightened out."

"I just had a call from Chief Torrence out there." Granger leaned back in his chair and made a pyramid of his hands, a most typical gesture.

"Oh?" I asked politely.

"They're having trouble with a rash—more like an epidemic of obscene phone calls and there seems to be some Boston tie-up."

I remembered seeing the chief with "the guy from the telephone company." "What's the Boston angle?"

Granger leaned forward, reached for some notes. "It seems that some kook, or kooks, got hold of a Wellesley phone book and they're systematically going down the list. Nearly every house in town, as far as the chief figures. Sometimes he goes from the front of the book, sometimes from the back."

"Every house?" My eyebrows rose. "Wellesley is in the West Suburban listings along with Newton, Needham, Weston, and a bunch of other towns. Any complaints from those places?"

"Chief Torrence says no. He says there's a small, privately printed directory that's distributed throughout the town. Courtesy of some civic club. He figures whoever's making the calls could be using this."

I frowned. "Is it in general distribution?"

"Seems to be. To every address in the town. 'Course,

they could be using the West Suburban listings, but he thinks if they were, the thing would cover more ground."

"What's the ploy of the caller?"

"He—it's a he, maybe more than one—he claims he's a doctor doing a survey. His research, he says, calls for answers to a number of questions and he starts off nice enough, but pretty soon he gets into the interviewee's sex life. You know how that goes. Chief Torrence says some of the ladies in the town are pretty upset."

"I can imagine. You say there's a Boston connection?"

"The telephone company has been doing its best to co-operate, but the caller has been jumping from locale to locale. Once they thought they had him, this was back at the start, a series of calls was traced to one Wellesley number. But then, they found out that the family who owned the house had been away for three months during the telephoning period. So they figured they'd set a trap, staked out the place for days. Nary a sign. The caller never came back."

"He broke into the house?"

"Through a cellar window. Never stole anything. Just used the phone."

I scowled. "Pretty cute."

"After that, he used pay booths and once, even, the telephone in the high school principal's office, don't know how he managed that. But the latest calls have been traced to—of all places—a phone booth at the Aquarium here."

"He does get around. How long has this been going on? There must be thousands of phones in Wellesley, literally."

"Close to a year now, according to the chief. He said he didn't know if the Aquarium booth would be used again, but he wondered if we could check it out. I said, sure, and, since you have a personal interest in the town, I thought maybe you and Parks were the men to do it."

"When does he telephone? Is there a time element involved?"

"It can be any day of the week. Never at night, always during the day. Chief Torrence calculates that's because he knows the housewife is alone at that time."

"If a man answers, hang up. Want us to go over to the Aquarium now?"

"Might as well. I don't know what to tell you to look for, but keep an eye open. If anything urgent comes up here, we'll call you back."

I nodded, got up to go. "Any voice description other than male?"

"Some say it's deep, some say on the high side. That's why the chief isn't sure whether it's one or more. He says the age is indeterminate, neither young nor old."

"Any chance it might really be a doctor? Perverted, but still a doctor?"

Granger shrugged. "Your guess is as good as mine. Minds get twisted in any profession."

"And who knows what a twisted mind looks like?" I started for the door. "Shall I report back to you—or Torrence?"

"If it's no go, it might be good for inter-police relations to let him know we made the effort. You be the judge. I can do it if you like."

"No sweat," I said. "I can stop by on my way home."

"Not a smell," I told Chief Torrence. "We hung around all day and came up with seventeen kids aged from twelve to sixteen or so, four women, a telephone repairman, trouble with vandals, and one elderly man calling his allergist. He said he'd found he was allergic to fish."

Chief Torrence looked grim. "I'm sorry I sent you on a wild goose chase. He's found a new location again. He called today from a pay booth in Dedham."

"How'd they trace that so quick?"

He looked even grimmer. "They didn't. We can anticipate him some because he seems to go right down the rows, but following it through to the other end isn't a matter of seconds. And he's got wind of the tracer, apparently, and now he's telling his victims where he's calling from. The law be damned, catch me if you can. I'd like to catch him—damn his dirty hide."

"Well"—I got ready to make my goodbyes—"I'm sorry we couldn't come up with anything. Let us know if there's anything else we can do."

"You live here, you said. On Howe Street?" His eyes were sharp and penetrating. From long years of trying to see into people's heads.

"That's right."

"Do you know Rudolph Wharton?"

"I know of him. I've seen him, but we haven't met."

"He's a selectman and, as such, one of my bosses. Being plagued by a different kind of maniac. A poison-pen letter nut."

I thought maybe I'd better not say that Dennehy had told me. "Is that so?"

"If you see anything around his place that looks funny

—you're trained, you'd have better eyes than the run-of-the-mill neighbor, let me know about it pronto, will you?"

He drummed the fingers of one hand on his desktop, a nervous drumming. "It doesn't look good when we can't solve the problem of a selectman."

"What are the letters about?"

He hesitated, turned his swivel chair and opened a file drawer behind him. "Read 'em yourself."

There were, as Dennehy had said, a dozen or so postmarked one week apart. They were pretty much the same in content, only the clipped and pasted words were printed differently.

They were addressed to both Wharton and to the chief, some of each.

The message was:

RUDOLPH WHARTON HAS MURDERED HIS WIFE AND HIDDEN HER BODY. IT IS BURIED SOMEWHERE IN HIS HOUSE OR ON HIS PROPERTY. YOU MAY THINK YOU CAN GET AWAY WITH MURDER RUDOLPH WHARTON BUT YOU CAN'T. I WON'T LET YOU.

And it was signed: THE GREAT EYE

It was almost ludicrous, or would have been if it weren't so ugly. "Somebody out there sure doesn't like him." I handed the letters back. "Where is the wife?"

"They're separated and she's gone to California. When these began to come he wrote to her and told her and she wrote to me." He passed me another sheet of paper. "Here's what the lady has to say. And we know it's her handwriting, Wharton attests to it."

I read this one. *Dear Chief Torrence, Rudolph has written me regarding the dreadful letters he has been receiving. This is to inform you that I am alive and kicking and to urge you to apprehend this miscreant—miscreant isn't strong enough a word by half—as soon as possible!*

She had signed it, *Sincerely, Ernestine Wharton,* and had added her Riverside, California, address.

I said slowly, "I don't know the man, of course, but I don't suppose this could be a fake . . ."

The chief shook his head emphatically. "I've learned to be overly suspicious, too, God knows. So I telephoned her. Paid for it myself, didn't want it to show up on the department phone bills. The selectmen have to approve the monthly vouchers. She's there all right and let me have what-for for not coming up with an answer."

I studied the fronts of the envelopes. Letter-by-letter pasted on. From Natick, as Dennehy had said. "Have the Natick police found out anything?"

"No. There are postal boxes all over town, of course. And they're just as busy as we are, maybe more, can't stand by all of them and they can't look at everybody's letters as they drop them in."

"No, of course not. But a glimpse of a pasted-up address should be enough . . . the postal police onto it?"

He took a deep breath. "Oh, yes. Nobody's spotted the bloody things at all until they end up inside the post office for cancellation and sorting. And then, they're bound by law to deliver them."

"I'll do what I can," I said doubtfully. I didn't see what I could do. Unless the Great Eye came calling.

Chief Torrence read my mind.

"I know," he told me. "I'm just grasping at straws.

Wharton's okay, he doesn't lay on me. But I know damn' well what he's thinking."

"I hope I can help," I told him, offering my hand. "I owe you a favor anyway. You did one for me once. You loaned Dennehy to me a few years back."

"Oh? Yes. Well, thanks." He didn't remember, but that was all right. A police chief or a police captain's got a lot on his mind.

At the door, I had a final thought. "Could I have a copy of those phone calls, times and places? Maybe I could puzzle over it in my spare time. And while you're at it, a copy of those letters, too."

"A copy? Sure. I'll get Elihu to Thermofax them for you. And we'll give you a copy of that special phone book, too. Maybe you'll see something in it that we haven't." And as he picked up his phone, I nodded and went out. Elihu was already working the copying machine when I got to the desk and when he gave me the list and a small paperback book entitled Wellesley Phone Numbers I thanked him and told him to say hi to Dennehy for me. He said he would.

Coming in through the back door of the house, I heard voices. "Knute, is that you?" Brenda called from the living room. "Come in and meet Mrs. Farley."

Mrs. Farley was a faded blonde wearing a red pants suit and drinking coffee with my wife. "I live right across the street," said Mrs. Farley offering her hand. "I thought it was about time I came over to say hello. I work for the local newspaper, the *Townsman*, but that doesn't mean I shouldn't make time to say hello to new neighbors. Late but sincere, that's me."

"We're invited to a party," Brenda told me. "Isn't that nice of Mrs. Farley?"

"Gloria. Please call me Gloria. We're having a few people in Saturday night for a buffet supper. Do hope you can come."

"Thanks." I looked at Brenda, got the message that she'd like to go. "What time?"

"Oh, about six-ish?"

"I don't usually get home until close to seven. Saturday's a working day for me, I'm afraid."

"Of course. That's all right. Come when you can, we'll be there. We won't eat until eight or so anyway." She put down her coffee cup, collected her cigarettes and matches. "I'd better be going. I've got to start dinner for the kids and Arlen, and I'm sure you have dinner to get, too. It's nice to have new neighbors. Especially compatible ones."

"She means as opposed to Mr. Wharton and Mercy Bird," Brenda explained when Gloria Farley had gone. "She says Mr. Wharton is a stuck-up town-father type and Mercy is funny, not ha-ha, but like a nut."

"Stuck-up. That's a good old-fashioned word. What's for dinner?"

"Meat loaf. But it will be a good hour."

"That's okay. I've got some home work to play with. How are you feeling?"

She smiled and hugged me. "Fat and sassy. Want a beer?"

"Uh-hum." I patted her behind, mimicked a TV commercial, "You're a good wife, Brenda."

And she came back with the pat answer, "I know."

Chief Torrence was right about the obscene phone call list. It was hard to find a handle. Just when I thought I had a thread—four calls on consecutive Mondays from a pay booth outside the Wellesley railroad station, between the hours of 8:30 and 9:30, could be a commuter? Then the pay booth number dropped from the list and was never used again.

Sometimes he called four-five days in a row and other times a week, even two went by without a complaint. That could mean, I supposed, that the callees hadn't been bothered sufficiently to report the calls, but it could also mean he didn't make any during that time.

"Brenda," I called, "have you got an old calendar around anywhere? Didn't I see one in one of those thousands of boxes?"

"The one I saved for the picture? I mean to frame it when I get around to it . . . yes, I think so. But I don't remember . . ."

"Well, never mind."

"Wait, I think maybe . . . down in the basement, there's a couple of boxes of odds and ends that we don't need right away . . ."

"Okay. I'll go look."

She laughed. "Let me go. You know you can never find anything."

"A fine recommendation for a cop," I muttered. She was so right.

"Well, you know it's true . . ." Her voice faded away and I heard her going down the cellar stairs. She came up again promptly, brought me a last year's calendar with a colored photograph of a New England covered bridge. "What are you saving that for?"

"It reminds me of home. New Hampshire."

"Well, all I want is the calendar."

"Be my guest. Want another beer?"

"I guess so." I started with the past June, the first of the calls, and began to write them in the squares. Maybe it would look different written out day by day.

No weekend calls, none at all. That fitted the theory that he called when the husband was unlikely to be at home. Husband. Did that mean he only called married women? If so, how did he know they were married? The phone book, of course. Call John Jones. "Is this Mrs. Jones?" Don't call Mary Jones. But why not? I wrote myself a note to ask the chief if all the women called were married.

Monday through Friday calls. Usually between nine and four. None during the noon hour. Three the first week. Two the second. Six the third. An even dozen the fourth week. None the fifth. That took him into July.

Only one call the sixth week. None the seventh and eighth. On vacation?

In August, he'd started slowly again. Two calls. Then three calls. None. Then in September, after school started, a big jump. Twenty-two calls the week after Labor Day week. A very busy boy that second week in September. And not a school boy. No opportunity once classes started. No, if he'd been a kid the summer months would have been his prime time.

"Knute, call Mein, will you? He's outside somewhere. And dinner's just about ready."

"Okay." Absent-mindedly, I tapped my pen against

my teeth as I headed for the front door. "Mein! Hey, cat." Obscene phone callers made me nervous. Evidence of a very sick mind, in my opinion. First phone calls, then maybe Peeping Toms and then . . .

"He's over here, I believe. Is this your feline fellow?"

The voice, masculine, came from across the street. I looked over to see a man with a lawn spreader and, at his feet, rubbing against a chino-trousered leg was Mein making kitten eyes at Rudolph Wharton.

I went over. "I didn't think he'd cross the street. My name's Severson. You're Mr. Wharton?"

"Right." We shook hands. He had interesting dark eyes, very bright and penetrating. "I'm afraid it's my fault. I like cats and he's such a handsome fellow. I lured him over."

I picked Mein up. He began to purr. "As long as he doesn't bother you. Some people aren't cat lovers . . ."

"Perfectly all right. As I said, I like cats. Used to have one, miss him. Getting settled in, are you? I've seen you and your wife working like Trojans."

"Yes, thanks. Bit by bit. It will take time, though. We lived in an apartment in Boston. This is quite a change." Mein began to knead at my shoulder.

"Understand you're on the Boston Police Force."

"That's right. Detective First Grade."

"Well, welcome to Wellesley. Our crime is of the minor variety, by and large." He released the handle of the spreader. "Care to come in for a drink?"

"Thanks, but dinner's on the table. And this fellow needs to eat, too." I stroked Mein's head. "I'll take a rain check if I may."

"Anytime." Wharton's smile was somewhat surprising.

It lit his long, dark-complexioned face. When I told Brenda about the encounter, she nodded.

"He sounds nice and he looks nice. He's quite a good-looking man."

"He is?"

"Well, I think so. Sort of a cross between Henry Fonda and Cary Grant."

I shook my head. "The ideas you women get. Anyway, he seems like a pleasant, friendly guy. I don't know why Gloria Farley and Mercy Bird are so down on him."

"Maybe he doesn't like them either," said Brenda.

"Where is Mercy, by the way? Haven't seen her lately. Only Algernon, looking mournful at the end of his chain."

"Working on a book she told me. 'I won't be around for a week or two,' she announced. 'I just hibernate when I'm working. See you when I get done.'"

I could just hear her saying it. Right to the point, that was Mercy Bird. "I wonder whose murder she's plotting now."

Brenda shook her head. "I went down to the library and got two of her books," she told me.

"Are they any good?" I asked.

"Haven't read them yet. She uses a pseudonym, you know."

"How'd you find out what it was?"

"The librarian told me."

"What name does she write under?"

"Tobias Wells."

"Oh," I said. "I think I've heard of her."

There were half a dozen people in the high-ceilinged living room when we got there. It wasn't a large room to begin with, the stairway cut into one side of it and a baby grand piano wearing a fringed scarf took up a good part of a small bay. Gloria, clad in a black silk ankle-length dress, or pants, or whatever it was with no back, was dispensing drinks from the top of the grand piano. "Hi, Seversons," she caroled. "Come name your poison." At that moment a motor whirred somewhere and a chair carrying a man slid down the wall side of the staircase, deposited its passenger neatly on the bottom tread.

"Greetings," said the electric chair rider. He was a big-chested man with a full head of wavy white hair and a mouthful of sparkling white teeth.

"Arlen," Gloria spoke without taking her attention from her bartending duties, "this is Brenda and Knute Severson, my husband. You've met our daughter Delilah, she let you in. And this pair on my right, Seversons, are Chris and Christine Beal. Christopher married Christine. Isn't that cute? And this is Harvey and Angela Klett and Dolly Selene. Say hello, everybody."

We did and I watched Arlen Farley get out of his stair chair and walk toward us. He walked a bit stiffly, but seemed to be all right in the legs. I wondered what was the reason for the stair chair and, reading my mind, Arlen told me.

"Had a coronary last year," he said jovially, reaching out his hand. "The doctor recommended this chariot. Actually, it's kind of fun."

"It makes a grand entrance," I told him, shaking hands. The three of us went to the piano bar. I found myself standing next to the woman Gloria had called Dolly Selene. She was maybe forty with silky auburn hair hanging down her back and around her shoulders. Her skin, and quite a good deal of it was visible above the top of her low-cut green dress, looked edible, definitely creamy.

"You're the Farleys' new neighbors," she told me. Her mouth was on the pouty side with a tendency to turn down at the corners except when she smiled as she did now. "I'm a couple of streets down. The corner of Weston Road and Avon."

"The big house? It's gray, isn't it?"

"That's it. A big house for one person. I'm a widow." She looked at me with wide green eyes.

"That's too bad," said Brenda politely.

Dolly sighed. Her chest expansion grew even larger when she sighed. "Yes. Robert passed away this spring. Thank God for friends like Gloria and the bunch from the little theater. Nobody wants a poor old widow on their hands." The green eyes looked mournful.

"Turn off the power, Dolly." The woman beyond her, Angela Klett if I remembered rightly, was small and thin with gray-brown hair cut short and shaggy. "You'll scare them off." To Brenda she said, "Dolly can't help it. She was born a femme fatale. But she doesn't mean it."

My, my, kitty, pull in your claws, I thought, but Dolly laughed easily. I gathered they knew each other well, well enough to take and give a dig without animosity. Listening to bits of conversation, it seemed they were all members of the same club, a little theater group. Probably that explained it.

Arlen Farley, accepting a ginger ale from his wife, explained, "Had to get off the hard stuff. Gave up the cigarettes, too." His many teeth gleamed. "The penalty for a misspent youth. Gloria tells me you're a detective."

I tasted my Scotch and soda, nodded. "What's your business?"

"Prosthetics."

"Prosthetics?"

"False teeth." He laughed and I wondered if he wore his own product. "Prosthodontists order choppers from me."

"Honestly, Arlen!" Gloria turned from a conversation with the Beals and Harvey Klett, made a face at her husband. "Choppers!"

Arlen grinned and reached in his coat pocket, brought something out hidden in his hand, placed it on the piano top where it clattered at us from a paisley background. A set of those joke teeth, clicking evilly away. "Oh . . ." Brenda, startled, moved back and everybody laughed, some more heartily than others.

"Put those away," Gloria commanded, eyes cast heavenwards. "He's got to pull that trick on everybody at least once."

"Don't be a wet blanket," Arlen told her. "If you don't make a joke about my business, you're what's known as a dull tool."

The front door opened and closed and a tall young man with a great deal of sandy hair and a straggly beard came in, followed by the girl Delilah, a symphony in blue denim if you could call such a closed-faced youngster a symphony, and stood looking at us. "Oh, Gregg." Gloria moved quickly to meet him. There was something tense about her voice, the way she moved. "Come in and meet the new neighbors. Severson, this is our son, Gregg."

"Hi." Said sullenly. This was then the dropout son as somebody had described him. He started up the stairs followed by his sister.

"Where have you been all day?" asked his mother, watching him climb.

"Riding around. I'm going right out again. Turk's waiting in the car for me."

"Where are you going?" she called after the disappearing figures.

"I don't know. Hacking around." A door opened, shut. She turned back to us with a wan smile.

"These kids," she said with a helpless gesture.

"Mr. Severson"—Dolly Selene was at my elbow again —"the funniest thing happened to me the other day."

"Knute," I corrected her. Now it would come, a story about a cop who stopped her for speeding when she wasn't going more than thirty miles an hour . . .

"Knute." Her full lips turned up into a smile. I had to

think of it as a seductive smile. "I had a dirty phone call. Can you imagine? At my age?" She smiled again.

"When was this?" I asked, all ears.

"Yesterday? No, the day before. He asked for Robert, the phone's still under Robert Selene, I thought I'd leave it that way. I said, stiffly, that Robert wasn't there. Then I waited to see what he'd say next. I mean, I wasn't going to tell him my husband was dead, not without finding out who he was."

"Who was he? Did he say who he was?"

"He said he was a Dr. Venable. Taking a survey on marriage. He said inasmuch as my husband wasn't in, I could help him with the survey. I said all right. I wasn't doing anything except watching a rather awful soap opera and, besides, I like surveys. Anyway, it was nice to talk to someone . . . it gets kind of lonely . . ."

Everyone was listening now. "What did he say then?" asked Christine Beal, a sweet-faced blonde.

"Well, at first he asked things like how long I'd been married, how long we'd dated beforehand, things like that. The kind of questions you'd expect, you know. But then . . ." She paused, clearly enjoying the attention.

"And then?" asked Gloria breathlessly.

"Then he wanted to know . . . some very personal things." Eyes cast down. "Like how many times . . ." She giggled.

"What did you say?" Angela's question was quick.

"I said, is this necessary? And he said, oh, yes, it's a very important part of the survey, I assure you. He said that all this information would be fed into a computer, no identification at all, just anonymous information. And I

said, Well, I don't know, and he said, Look, if you'll
finish the survey I'll put you on my paid subject list and I
said what in the world is a paid subject and he said persons who are particularly helpful get paid. It's only twenty
dollars, he said, but that he'd give me an address and if
I sent a self-addressed envelope, he'd send me a check."

"Dolly, how could you be so gullible?" Christine Beal
looked appalled and her balding husband added, "I
hope you didn't do it."

Dolly bridled. "Of course I did. He already had my address from the phone book, didn't he? If I was going to
go to all that trouble, I might as well get paid for it. After
all, insurance is insurance but it's not as though Robert
left me independent for life."

"Go on," I urged. "He began to ask about your sex life.
Then what?"

"Well, it got even more personal after that. Back to my
childhood sex habits. And the years in between. Not only
how often, but how, if you know what I mean. With
graphic descriptions. I began to get very uncomfortable,
to tell you the truth, but I'd gone so far already . . . and
then the questions got worse and worse and I said to
him, 'Look, what are you, a dirty old man?' I really did
say that." She nodded her head emphatically.

"What did he answer?" It must be the same one. I
didn't know if Chief Torrence had received as complete
a report as Dolly was giving. Or, if the women who had
complained had listened to "Dr. Venable" as long as
Dolly Selene had.

"There was a long silence. I thought I'd made him angry, to tell you the truth, but then he laughed, a sort of

cackling laugh, and he said, 'Mrs. Selene, I would like to meet you. I really would.' "

"Meet you?" Christine looked horrified.

"Oh, I wouldn't, of course. I told him that. And I told him I wouldn't answer any more questions. He thanked me, then, and just before he hung up he said he might be calling me again."

I frowned. That didn't fit the pattern. Perhaps it was just a goodbye line, none of the complainants had reported a repeat call, I was sure of that. But suppose he did call her again—what a break! The telephone company might be able to trace it, a bug on her line . . . or, if not trace, at least we could listen in, maybe pick up a voice, a way of speaking . . . "Did he have an accent of any kind? Anything unusual? What sort of voice did he have?"

"Well, quite deep, silky. I'd call it . . ." She giggled again. "To tell you the truth, I'd call it a sexy voice."

"Did you report this to the police?"

Wide-eyed. "Well, no. At first I thought it was legitimate, you see."

Angela murmured, "Dolly, you never were the Phi Beta Kappa type."

Dolly looked hurt. "That isn't fair, Angela. Things are a lot freer now, you know, people say things they never thought of saying a few years back. And doctors do have to ask embarrassing questions. What would you do?"

"I would have hung up."

"Well, I didn't. But what I did do then was to look his name up in the phone book. He'd given me this address, you see. And he wasn't in the book, not in the white pages or the yellow. So then I thought, maybe he has an unlisted phone. If you call information and ask, they'll tell you if someone has, you know. But information said there was no phone at all at that address, there were no unlisted Venables, that there were only six Venables in all the greater Boston phone books and none of them was a doctor. So then I began to wonder if it hadn't been just a dirty phone call."

Angela's eyebrows rose. "You began to wonder?"

"There have been a lot of them in recent months," Gloria said slowly. "We wanted to make a big thing of it in the paper, to get people to report to the police, maybe then they could catch him, but the chief was afraid it would simply inspire a rash of obscene calls from all the nuts so we soft-pedaled it."

"I'd like to report this call to the Wellesley police," I told Dolly Selene. "It is one of a series as Gloria said. Would you mind? They will probably come and ask you questions. Or you could go down to the station . . ."

"Well, no, I wouldn't mind. I didn't even think to . . . but then I didn't know about the others. Tell them if you want to." She gave Angela an arch glance. "I'll be glad to be of help."

"There's a good chance you can be," I assured her.

"Well, speaking of police, I've got a better story for you," Chris Beal spoke up. "I was driving in on Route 9, about 40 miles an hour, and this State cop . . ."

"What a dreadful woman," muttered Brenda, closing the front door on the fine, but still somewhat chilly spring air.

"Who?" I covered a yawn. I was tired, quite ready to go to bed.

"That Dolly Selene. She may be a widow and all that, but I cannot stand that sort of casting the bait upon the waters."

Mein came up to rub against me and I told him, "I suppose you must go out." To Brenda I said, "Casting the bait? I don't get it."

"Of course you don't!" she flung at me, headed for the kitchen. After I let the cat out, I found her closing the refrigerator, pouring a glass of milk.

"Make that two," I said mildly. I was anxious to hear more. Sounded to me like a virulent case of jealousy and never since I'd known her had I known Brenda to be jealous of me. Once it was the other way around.

She spilled some milk in the pouring, fussed under her breath as she wiped it up. "What did Dolly Selene do to get your back up?" I asked with interest.

"All that nonsense about she didn't realize it was an obscene phone call. So anxious to talk to a man, any man, she didn't care what he said to her."

"Maybe so." I took a long drink of milk. Uhmmm, good after all that liquor. "But why should that make you so up tight?"

"It makes me ashamed of women, that's what. Clinging vine-types with all bosoms showing."

I grinned at her. "Now, now. I wouldn't say you were exactly flat-chested. Especially now."

To my astonishment, she burst into tears. "I know I look terrible."

"You don't look terrible . . ."

"I know I'm fat and ugly and it just goes on and on and I'm so damned tired of looking like this and that woman just stood there, snuggling up to you and making cow's eyes . . ."

I put my arms around her, or rather I started to. She jerked away. "Brenda, darling . . . you're just tired to-night, don't get yourself all unhappy, you look wonderful to me. I didn't pay any attention at all to Dolly Selene . . ."

"You spent all evening talking to her!"

My temper flared at the unjust accusation. "I didn't spend all evening talking to her. I only listened to the phone call story and that's because I talked to the chief here about them, it's business, and besides, I had to be polite to the woman, didn't I?"

"Polite!" she snapped, drained her milk and set the glass angrily into the sink. "I suppose you call staring down her cleavage all night being polite."

"Brenda"—I tried to keep my tone conciliatory—"you're being unreasonable. I couldn't care less about the woman, she's much too old for me in the first place and in the second place, I happen to have a very good wife of whom I'm rather fond . . ."

"Fond! Of course. You never have loved me, all those years you just tolerated me and then when you were getting to the point where you thought it might be politic to get married, I was the only one around . . ."

"Damn it, that isn't so and you know it. Stop this! You don't sound like Brenda Severson at all, you sound like a fishwife."

"A fishwife! How would you know what a fishwife sounds like . . . if Dolly Selene sounded like a fishwife, that wouldn't bother you, would it . . ."

"Brenda!" This time I reached out and caught her, shook her gently. "Honey, just calm down. Come to bed. You'll feel better in the morning."

"I won't feel better in the morning. I won't feel better until this baby is born. My back hurts and I can hardly get out of a chair and I look like some grotesque . . ."

"Shhh, shhh," I whispered and held her close. She cried a little but stopped talking. "Come on," I said softly, turning her. "Up to bed. I'll never see or even talk to Dolly Selene again, I promise you, come on, darling, you're tired and you'll feel so much better . . ."

She pulled away from me. "Damn it, Knute, stop patronizing me. I'm just going through a late-pregnancy syndrome." And head high, she marched out of the kitchen and up the stairs.

I sighed and went to the door to call Mein. The perverse creature wouldn't come, of course. Out looking for a girl friend, no doubt. Which just goes to show that some males never learn even after an operation.

I had another glass of milk to give Brenda time to get into bed. I was too tired to indulge further in any more arguments and besides, oddly enough, I could understand a little of what she felt.

I was just finishing the milk when the telephone rang. I picked up the receiver of the phone on the kitchen wall, thinking now what? A woman's voice said breathlessly, "Mr. Severson? This is Dolly Selene."

I heard the upstairs receiver go down. Brenda must have picked it up just as I did, heard the caller identify herself. Oh, boy. I said cautiously, "Yes, Mrs. Selene. What can I do for you?"

"Dolly. You were going to call me Dolly."

"Yes. Dolly, of course."

"I hate to disturb you at this hour, but I thought perhaps you'd still be awake. I just got home myself and I've been thinking about that phone call. It was stupid of me, but I didn't realize it was one of many, I just thought it was rather funny, you know, humorous at the time, but now I'm rather . . . well, not frightened, but nervous. I would really like to talk to you about it. Perhaps you could drop by my house tomorrow sometime. I'd be happy to give you a drink."

"I'm sorry, Mrs. . . . I mean, Dolly. I work tomorrow. But I'm sure Chief Torrence will send a man out to discuss it with you. It's actually his baby, you see." If I knew what was good for me, and I did, I planned never to go near the luscious Dolly Selene.

"Oh, dear. Of course. I didn't realize. Tell the chief I shall be home all day tomorrow then. No place else to go." She laughed wistfully. "And thank you for being so understanding."

I told her she was welcome. "And don't worry. Chief Torrence has some very able men. They'll take good care of you."

"Oh, I know. And I know it's silly, but when you're all alone . . ."

"You may never be bothered by the man again."

"I suppose not. Even though he said . . . I've been thinking, too, about his voice. You asked me about that and I hadn't really thought much about it but now I wonder . . ."

"You wonder what?"

"If at the beginning it didn't sound just the least little bit familiar. Nothing I can put my finger on, just a fragmentary impression."

I couldn't help it, I yawned. "Perhaps it will come to you after you've slept on it. Be sure and tell Chief Torrence, or whoever comes, about that." If she dwelt on it long enough, she could probably imagine anything . . . but maybe it really was someone she knew. I doubted it, she hadn't said a word about it when she'd told the story, more of an afterthought, an embellishment. And yet, I supposed it was possible. Obscene telephoners have to live in a world like the rest of us. They must have acquaintances, if not friends. Not impossible that she might be right. "Sleep on it," I suggested. "And don't leave anything out when the police come."

"All right." She laughed again, that sad little laugh.

"I'll have a nightcap and hit the lonely hay. Maybe it will come to me in a dream."

"Good night, Dolly. And thank you for calling." I didn't know what I was thanking her for, but as I'd told Brenda, I had to be polite.

"Good night, Knute. It was so nice to meet you. And your little wife."

When I got upstairs, the bedroom light was out and Brenda was, to all appearances, sleeping. I said, "She thinks she might have recognized the voice on the telephone."

No answer.

I remembered that Mein was still out, almost went down to try again to get him in, then thought to hell with it, to hell with all of it, and went to bed.

Dennehy's Sandi Smith was petite and bubbly. Dark-haired and dark-eyed, she came up to just below Dennehy's shoulder and she spent a great deal of time looking up at him wide-eyed. Obviously, he liked it and I thought I heard the faint caroling of wedding bells in the distance.

"I'll be so happy when I'm out of quarantine," Brenda was telling her. "I never knew nine months could be so long."

"Oh." Sandi looked starry-eyed now. "I think it's just wonderful. I'd like to have a baseball team."

"Anything new on the telephone call business?" I asked Dennehy.

"He's quieted down." Dennehy and I were drinking beer, I handed him a refill.

"Maybe he'll get tired of the game and call it off."

"Could be. I'd like to get him, though. The thing that bugs me is how he almost seems to know what we're up to. Like he had a pipe line, you know."

"A lead to the force, you mean?"

"Something like that. It spooks me. Somebody watching over my shoulder."

I nodded soberly. "Did Dolly Selene help any?" I thought Brenda glanced my way at that, but when I looked over she was reciting the tale of the making of the drapes to Sandi who seemed properly impressed.

"No. She's a little strange, that one. It's hard to tell how much she adds to the story whenever she tells it. The chief says she'd like it if we adopted her down at the station. She's taken to dropping in." He grinned, lowered his voice. "I think she's got the hots for Dorsey."

I laughed. "What does Dorsey say to that?"

"He just groans and goes off on a fishing trip."

"Has Wharton got any more letters?"

Dennehy shook his head. "Which reminds me, there's an opening for sergeant and I'm pretty high on the civil service list. They've asked me to come before the selectmen for an interview."

"Is that the way they pick a sergeant?"

"Yes, two or three of us get called in and they talk to us father and son like and then they make up their minds. It's set for Monday and I'm nervous as hell."

"Don't worry, Kevin. They'll pick you." Sandi beamed over at him.

"I've never been to a selectman's meeting," I told Dennehy.

"Why don't you come down Monday? Give me moral support. I'm due at 8 P.M. Can you make it?"

I shook my head. "I go on nights next week. I'm sorry, Dennehy. But I'll keep my fingers crossed for you."

"He hasn't got a thing to worry about," said Sandi

Smith with certainty. "I looked up his horoscope and it's all there."

"I wish I were as sure as you are," Dennehy told her. He glanced backward through our picture window. "I wish I knew how that fellow over there was going to vote."

I followed his gaze. Rudolph Wharton's house was dark except for a dim light in the living room. That was often the way, I assumed he sat there night after night in the semidarkness and watched television. A lonely man for all his money and power. I had a wry thought, I should introduce him to Dolly Selene. Only, he had a wife. A dead wife, according to the letter writer. Why in God's name would somebody write letters like that about something that was so patently untrue? That, to me, was the most interesting part of the puzzle. One day, when I had time, I'd talk to him about it. Someone with a most peculiar mind wished him ill. The letter writer and the telephone caller—two very warped personalities.

They'd make quite a pair if they ever got together.

And wouldn't it be something if they were one and the same? I stared at my empty beer glass. Wild idea. Much too farfetched. But wouldn't it be something?

"I don't understand your interest in this nasty business." Rudolph Wharton's eyes were not friendly, his expression was cold.

"I know, it's none of my affair." I hitched myself forward on his sofa. His living room had the look of a womanless house, clean, but not cared for. "I guess you can just put it down to once a cop, always a cop. I did a little poking on these obscene telephone calls for the chief and that got me interested in that angle. And I got to thinking, the psychology of the caller and the letter writer is somewhat the same. Anonymity . . . mischief . . . perversion. I just thought if you wouldn't mind telling me about the letters, we might find a connection of some sort. The calls started before the letters, a year ago. And the first letter came early this year . . ."

"Right after my wife left." His voice was stiff.

"Have you given any thought as to why the letter writer would accuse you of something completely invalid? I mean, it would be more reasonable if your wife had gone on, say, a trip around the world where she couldn't be reached and where it would be hard to prove her alive or dead?"

"Of course it would be more reasonable. But the letter writer is not reasonable, not reasonable in any sense of the word." He made an effort to be gracious. "Can I get you something to drink? A highball?"

A drink might relax him. "If you'll join me."

He nodded curtly, took my order. I studied the room further. The furniture was of good quality, but unimaginative. Beige walls, pale carpet, tannish covered couch, pale green chair and leather man's chair. Books in bookshelves bound in dull red leather. Stack of magazines. On top, *Life*, latest issue. I nudged it with my forefinger. Underneath, *Playboy?* By God it was. I moved *Life* back into place. He was human after all.

His voice preceded him from the kitchen as he returned, bearing drinks. "I was reluctant to express any suspicions to Chief Torrence. In my position, you see, it would be so easy to point a finger and be wrong. And now that the letters have ceased—there hasn't been one in two or three weeks now—I'm glad I didn't. Now that he's seen that his insane hoax didn't work, he's let it die."

I took my glass. "Thank you. But surely you want him caught, nonetheless? You said your suspicions . . . you have an idea who it might be?"

He looked at me blankly. "If I do, I'd rather keep it to myself. If I am incorrect, I could cause a great deal of harm."

I frowned at him. "If you are correct and don't follow through, you could do a great deal more harm. A person who's that deranged—and deranged he must be—is capable of more than writing letters."

Wharton sighed. "I know. I've wrestled with it ever since it started, believe me. But I have no evidence, none at all. It's just a hunch, because of the situation, you see. And because of . . . well, he is especially vulnerable."

I tasted the drink, it was on the weak side. If he hadn't said anything to Chief Torrence about his suspicions, why was he hinting of them to me? And furthermore, if he had a hunch as he put it, wouldn't it be natural for him to tell the chief? His own police chief? A man he certainly must trust? For the first time, I began to wonder about Rudolph Wharton, about his part in this little mystery. Could he be writing the letters himself? For God's sake, for what reason?

"On the other hand," I spoke easily, a philosophic conversation, "if you do have an idea and you let the police check it out, they could clear him, whoever he is, if you are, as you fear, incorrect."

He stared into his glass. "Yes, I suppose that is true. If I explain a bit—you see, he was very fond of my wife. Unusually so. And she was kind to him. I rather imagined that when she left so abruptly, he missed her perhaps even more than I. I thought at first, he has imagined this because he is so hurt at her leaving. But then the letters continued and I knew he was purposefully castigating me."

"He was fond of your wife. And she was kind to him. It must have been someone you—and she—saw often." We were going to play guessing games? All right with me.

"Well, yes, of course. It's a little hard to avoid . . . yes." He finally took a sip from his drink.

"You were going to say to avoid . . . a relative?" Watching his face, I felt as though I was playing Charades. Not a relative. "A close friend?" I didn't think so. "A business associate?" Possible, but . . . "A neighbor?"

Bingo. "Look, Severson, I don't want to get the boy into trouble. He's at that age when things are difficult enough, I remember my own teen years . . ."

"Gregg Farley? The boy next door? You think Gregg Farley has been writing those letters?"

He made a helpless gesture. "As I told you, I have no evidence. He hasn't been attending school this spring. I'd guess he dropped out just about the time that Ernestine—left. He's a difficult boy, I know his parents are quite upset about him. He hardly communicates with them at all, but Ernestine had some sort of way that he responded to. She encouraged him, listened to him. Many's the time I'd come home and find them together. I couldn't understand her interest, if you want to know the truth. I consider him a churlish boy. But I suppose it was because she always wanted children and we never had any . . ."

"The cut-up words, where could he have done that? And the trips to Natick?"

"There's no one home during the day, you know. Arlen is at his place of business, Gloria works at the *Townsman* and the girl, Delilah, is in school. There's no reason that he couldn't have composed the letters, and he has a motorbike. Very simple to run it to Natick, put them in the mailboxes."

Alone during the day and a dropout from school. With a motorbike. Time to form letters and time to make phone calls, too. Even from the high school office? Who better than a student waiting for the principal. But the calls came last fall, and Wharton had said he'd dropped out when his wife left. "Had he ever played hookey before? Before he dropped completely out?"

Wharton rotated his glass between his hands. "I suppose so. I don't really know. He didn't confide in me—and neither did Ernestine toward the last."

Toward the last. A final sounding phrase. "Maybe it would be wise to get in touch with Mrs. Wharton—to ask her about the boy."

He looked up at me, a brightness in his eyes that I took to be pain. "I'd rather not."

I stared at him.

His lids dropped. "She—the parting was most unfriendly. I had to take my hat in hand to beg her to write and say that she was well. I would prefer not to ask more favors."

Proud and cold. Gloria Farley had called him stuck-up. "Then what you prefer to do is . . . ?"

A direct gaze again. "Let the thing drop. Except for personal annoyance, no one has been hurt. Give the boy time to get over his aberrations. It could be his age. It could be a passing thing. I say, let it slide."

I'd met his kind before. The "I don't want to cause any trouble, I've got my money back, let it go" variety of public-spirited citizen. And they burned me, God, how they burned me. Because whoever they let go nine times out of ten went right out and did the same or worse again. And I couldn't help saying to Selectman Rudolph Wharton who should have known better, "Until the next time."

I'll give him this, though. He looked abashed. "It's just that he's seventeen . . . old enough to have a mark on his record and too young to really understand what's right and what's wrong."

I put my unfinished drink down on his mahogany table, stood up. "As you say, there's no evidence," I told him. "And also, as you say, it's none of my business. I only hope, Mr. Wharton, that you're right and I'm wrong. Because we're both old enough to know the difference."

The baby was born on June 13—quite unexpectedly.

Parks and I went to court that day, two different courtrooms, two different cases where we'd been arresting officers.

Mine was an insurance fraud case. This twenty-year-old loaned his car to a teen-ager without a license, God knows why he loaned it, retarded was my guess. At any rate, the teen-ager smashed the front of the car up against a guard rail and the car owner came up with the bright idea that he'd ditch it someplace and declare it stolen. Only trouble was, there was a witness to the collision between the car and the guard rail and the witness got the license number and before the genius got the car stashed and reported stolen, Parks and I drove over to his house to check it out.

The boy's father was tear-assed. He knew who'd been driving the car, had seen him deliver it back in less than mint condition. So he ranted and raved to us about irresponsible drivers, never knowing, as it turned out, that the teen-ager had been an unauthorized operator of a motor vehicle.

In the meantime, the twenty-year-old was down at Division One describing his "stolen" vehicle. By the time we got the interested parties together, we had it pretty well sorted out. The insurance company, understandably, took a dim view. Which is why I was in court when Brenda got sharp and sudden labor pains two weeks too early.

I came back to Division after four that afternoon, hot, tired, hungry, and greatly irritated at sitting around half the day waiting for the case to be called. Davoren flagged me before I set foot inside the squadroom. "It's your wife," he told me excitedly. "She's gone to the hospital."

"Where? When?"

"The Newton-Wellesley. Just a little while ago, I guess. A Mrs. Farley called, said she and Mr. Wharton were driving her there . . ."

I took off without, I think, even thanking him. She wasn't due yet, Dr. Abraham had said only yesterday that things were going as per schedule . . . what had happened? Oh, God, I prayed, don't let anything be wrong!

I parked in the emergency zone, rushed in through the emergency door. They told me Brenda was in maternity, told me how to get there. The elevator wouldn't come, why the hell didn't they have more elevators in this place, and I gave up after a minute, began to run up the stairs that seemed to climb on and on.

Out of breath I pushed the door open on the maternity ward and ran into Rudolph Wharton standing by that elevator.

I grabbed him. "Brenda?"

"She's in the delivery room. The doctor's with her." He placed his hand on the side of the elevator door to keep it from closing. "I'll be right back, just going to move my car. I left it at the emergency door. Mrs. Farley's in the waiting room. She'll tell you all about it."

I let him go, mumbling, "Thanks," to his back. Gloria Farley was sitting in a chair, smoking a cigarette, looking completely calm. How could everybody be so relaxed? Didn't they realize that something could be—must be wrong?

"Surprise, surprise." Gloria beamed at me.

"What happened? Is Brenda all right? The baby . . . ?"

Gloria patted the seat beside her. "Just sit down and take a couple of deep breaths. Heavens, you look ashen. Your offspring decided it was time to come into the world, that's all. Didn't they tell you that at your office?"

I sat down. "I don't know. All I heard was Brenda and hospital, I didn't wait to hear more. But how could it be, two weeks early?"

"It happens that way sometimes. Doctors can miscalculate, you know. Here, have a cigarette."

"No, thanks. You're sure she's all right? She didn't fall or anything . . . ?"

"No, she didn't fall. She was out in the yard, planting some pansies. I was on my porch, finally found a moment to read the morning paper. I glanced over and saw Brenda kneeling there, I got the impression she couldn't get up. I was about to call over to her when Mr. Wharton drove up. Good thing he did, too. Arlen has the station wagon and Gregg took my car. Anyway, I went over and Brenda said, 'Gloria, I think the baby's coming. Coming quick.' So I said, 'Take it easy,' and helped her to her feet. I hailed Wharton and while he brought the car over, I called you and the doctor." She stubbed out her smoke in an ashtray, looked pleased with herself.

"Thanks. Thanks a million," I said sincerely as well as inadequately.

Gloria raised her pale eyebrows. "So what else are neighbors for?"

"Can I see Dr. Abraham? Has he spoken to you?"

"Just to say hello. He seems quite capable, I can tell you that. I don't know if you can see him now or not. The head nurse took him off. When she comes back you can ask. Oh, oh. This must be another one."

A round-faced man in a dark suit emerged from the elevator carrying a small suitcase. Which reminded me, had Brenda brought her things? She'd talked of packing a bag, but I wasn't sure whether she'd done it yet.

Round-face approached us, looked forlornly at the empty nurse's office. "Where is everybody? Does anybody know where my wife is?"

"They seem to be rather busy," Gloria Farley told him. "Sit down and join the party. Someone's sure to be back soon."

He pouted, he had the face for it. "Damn poor way to run a hospital."

"I take it your wife is having a baby. Mine, too." I introduced myself.

He put out his hand. "Dr. Phelps. Glad to meet you." Seating himself in a third chair, he seemed pretty cool.

"A doctor, huh? No wonder you're not crawling the walls. It's my first, I mean Brenda's first. And I don't know what's happening."

"I'm a dentist, not an M.D. And this is our fifth. Ursula always picks the middle of the day for some reason, usually when I'm in the middle of an extraction. So we've figured out a routine. She calls me and grabs a cab. I follow when I can. We're used to it." He sighed gently and leaned back in his chair. "This time the doctor says it's twins. That will make six, all under the age of eight."

Gloria shook her head in mock despair. "You'd better get the pill."

Phelps pulled a long face. "I don't believe in it."

The elevator doors swooshed open and Rudolph Wharton returned. "How's it coming?"

I shook my head. "No word." Where the devil were the nurses anyway? And even as I thought the thought, one of them emerged through double swinging doors at the end of the corridor. Phelps and I almost collided, trying to reach her first.

"Nothing yet," she told me in a businesslike voice. "Dr. Abraham is with her." To Phelps she said, "We've got a surprise for you, Dr. Phelps. Two girls and a boy. Born about twenty minutes ago."

His mouth opened, closed, opened again. "Triplets?" he asked, and then, "And one is a boy?"

"That's right." Her smile was as professional as her voice.

"Did you hear that, Severson?" He grabbed me excitedly. "A boy! At last, a boy. The other four are girls, you know. At last, a boy!" He turned to the nurse. "When can I see them?"

"In a little while, I'll let you know. And I'll let you know, too, Mr. Severson. As soon as I have any news."

"She's all right?" I insisted. "My wife, she's all right?"

"She's doing just fine." And the nurse went into her cubicle, leaving us standing and leaving me feeling like a young boy in the principal's office wondering what it was he had done.

"Yes, I really should get home, too," Gloria was saying to Wharton when I came back to them. "I've got a family to feed."

"There's no news yet," I told them.

"As long as you're here, would you mind if we left, Severson?" Wharton asked me. "There's a selectmen's meeting tonight."

"Of course not. I don't know how to thank the two of you."

"Glad to do it." Wharton put out his hand. "Let us know how it comes out."

I shook his hand heartily. "I will. And thanks again."

"No trouble at all."

Phelps came back and took Gloria's seat, fidgeted with his Masonic tie pin. "Frederick Ferdinand Phelps, the second," he murmured. He looked up. "I like the second better than junior, don't you?"

"Sounds all right to me." Leif, if it was a boy. Not Leif Ericson, of course. I'd been kidding when I said that and Eric the Red. Leif George for my father. But if it were a girl—we hadn't decided on a name for a girl.

"It's great news, simply great. A son. To carry on the

name. I was beginning to think . . . a son! God, how a man wants a son."

I nodded. I supposed I wanted a son, too. But actually, I was more concerned about Brenda and whether the baby would be all right than I was about its sex.

"It's the X and Y chromosomes, you know." Phelps nodded his head wisely.

"What? Oh, yes."

"I'd begun to wonder if Ursula's X chromosomes were so strong they were annihilating my Y chromosomes." He pushed his lower lip out, sucked it back and smiled. "But not this time. No, sir!"

As a conversational subject, I found chromosomes on the boring side. "What kind of dentist are you? Regular, or do you specialize?"

"Just a D.M.D." The lip came out again. "Thought of going into orthodontistry or endodontistry but the kids started coming right off . . ."

"The lady who was here with me, her husband is in a related field. Prosthetics. Maybe you know him. His name is Arlen Farley."

Phleps frowned a small frown. "Can't say that I do. What lab is he with? What does he do? Full plates? Partial dentures?"

"I'm not sure. I didn't know there was a difference."

"Certainly, certainly. Specialists in every field these days, you know. Different processes. Dentures, that is full plates are made from acryllics while partials are metal-based. Gold—or vitalium, mostly. Very skilled work, takes an artisan. You make a waxed pattern, you see, and then the metal is heated to two thousand degrees. Now, in crown or bridgework, that's another field, there are gold crowns, porcelain crowns, porcelain on gold—they use those on actors and such, very expensive but worth it if you're on TV or the stage . . ."

I found his dissertation on prosthetics almost as dull as his lecture on chromosomes. Where the devil was Dr. Abraham? What was taking so long? I looked over to the nurse. She was talking to somebody on the telephone.

Phelps's voice broke into my thoughts. ". . . a racket, you know. You have to be especially trained in one of the lab training schools. Have to know anatomy to begin with and then you have to know your materials. If the gold expands more than the porcelain, the porcelain cracks. Gold men have got to know their business and porcelain men have to be artists, know all about hue, warmth of tone. And these fly-by-nights, selling dentures at cut-rate prices, are bilking the public. Not that I'm insinuating your friend is one of those. The fact that I don't know him is insignificant, we all have our favorite laboratories. But these basement technicians, the Dental Society is after them, I can tell you. Put 'em behind bars, almost too good for them."

The nurse hung up the phone, looked over at us. "Dr. Phelps, you can go in now and see your wife. Room 233."

He stood eagerly, suitcase in hand. "And my son?"

"You can see the babies in the nursery after you've seen your wife."

As I watched him trot down the hall, I thought it was bright of the nurse to tell him where to go first. Unless I'd figured him wrong, he was more interested in the nursery than in Room 233.

Suddenly I wished I had a cigarette. I hadn't smoked

one in years, but I felt a terrible hunger for one in that
moment. Why did it take so long? Was Brenda in awful
pain? No, of course not. They'd give her something. We'd
talked about natural childbirth, but she was afraid of it
and I didn't blame her. She was thirty years old—was
that too old to start having children? Of course not, Dr.
Abraham had said. Brenda was healthy, he had said.
Damn it, why did it take so long?

The elevator doors opened and a man and a woman
stepped off. A very pregnant woman. They went over to
the desk, spoke to the nurse. I couldn't hear what they
were saying.

Brenda, are you all right? Brenda, dearest . . .

The elevator doors opened again, a gray-haired man
came out carrying a small doctor's bag. He joined the
group at the desk.

Another nurse came through the swinging doors at
the end of the corridor. I watched her come my way,
watched eagerly, but she stopped at the nurse's desk.

I found I was chewing a fingernail, took my hand from
my mouth.

I looked at my watch . . . 6:37. Why did it take so
long?

The couple and the doctor left the desk, went down the
hall with the other nurse. The man had his arm around
the woman's shoulders. I should have been with Brenda
when she came. I shouldn't have left her to come with
strangers. I looked at my watch again . . . 6:39. Why did
time drag so?

Concentrate on something else, I told myself. Try to
remember the new figures on crime in Boston—that
should be a good mental exercise. A hundred fourteen

murders last year (seventh in the nation), three hundred three rapes (tenth), three thousand three hundred twenty-one (was that right?) robberies, ranking seventh; ten thousand plus burglaries, tenth; aggravated assaults? I couldn't recall the exact amount, one thousand six hundred-some; and second in auto thefts, second in the whole country with well over fifteen thousand.

Right up there, my city. Right up there in the top ten.

But things were improving. What had the commissioner said? "If it weren't for our stolen car figures, we'd probably have the lowest crime rate of any major city in the U.S. The aggravated assault rate is 30 percent lower than cities of comparable size or larger; the robbery rate is 19 percent lower; the burglary figure is 25 percent lower . . ."

"Mr. Severson."

I nearly jumped from my seat. It was the businesslike nurse speaking to me from the desk. She had the phone to her ear.

"Yes?" I hurried forward.

She smiled, this time, I thought, more warmly. "You have a son. Born at 6:35. Weighing seven pounds, one ounce."

I gawked at her. "Is he—is my wife—all right?"

"Both mother and son are doing fine. You can see your wife in just a few minutes."

For the first time in my life I had to fight the urge to hug and kiss a 160-pound, slightly horse-faced, gray-haired, middle-aged woman.

So all I did was say, "Thank God."

I was talking to my mother on the telephone from home. "And Brenda is just fine. Honestly, to me she's never looked more beautiful. And wait till you see your new grandson! He looks just like a china doll. Bald as a billiard with big blue eyes and he's going to be tall, Dr. Abraham says he's long, twenty-one inches, that's considered long and . . ."

My mother laughed. "Oh, Knute, I've never heard you sound so happy. Your father and I are delighted, too, you know that."

"I told you what we named him, didn't I? Leif George, for Dad. Leif George Severson. Doesn't that sound right, absolutely right?"

"Yes, dear. It's a lovely name. Here, your father wants to talk to you. Now don't go on and on, George, you know this phone call from Boston is costing Knute money."

"Mom," I demurred and Dad's voice came on.

"Knute, m' boy. So I'm a grandfather at last!"

"Wait until you see him . . ." The doorbell rang.

"Your mother is telling me right now that you and Brenda should come here on your vacation."

"Dad, there's somebody at the door. Hold on a minute, will you?"

"I'll hang up, Knute. Like your mother said, long distance calls cost money. Write us and tell us when you're coming to Florida! Bye, Knute."

There was a click on the line and the doorbell pealed once more. "Damn," I said, hanging up the phone.

It was Mercy Bird at the door. She was wearing a nondescript-colored raincoat that hung to her ankles and a big, floppy felt hat, once colored orange, now sort of a salmon shade. She handed me a package all wrapped in Christmas paper as she said, "Congratulations. Here's a little present for the baby."

"Come in, Mercy. Come in. How in the world did you know? I thought you were incommunicado, writing."

"Don't you know I have ESP? And I do a lot of peeking out the window. How else can I keep up with things? I saw them go off in Wharton's car. Being nimble-minded, I put two and two together. When you came home looking as though you'd like to kick your heels in the air, I said, Mercy Bird, Knute Severson is a father."

"You're so right and I'm so glad to see you. I need someone to celebrate with. Come have a beer."

"You're sure I'm not interrupting something?"

"Not at all. How's my friend, big Algernon?"

"Getting bigger by the day, I'll swear. May I ask the state of Mein's health?"

"Fat and sassy. He's out, but chasing squirrels or lady cats, I can't say. Even though he's been—well, he still retains an interest." I took two beers from the refrigerator and opened them. I really was glad to see her.

"Now you save the present for Brenda to open," Mercy told me, accepting the beer. "You didn't tell me which it was, a boy or a girl?"

I grinned at her. "I thought you worked that out with your ESP."

She looked thoughtful. "I would have except that I don't think it mattered to you that much."

"It didn't, or at least I didn't think it did. Anyway, I'm pleased to report that Leif George Severson was born on this day."

Mercy smiled and lifted her beer can. I raised mine in return and thus we toasted the arrival of my son.

When she'd sipped from her can and put it down, Mercy said, "It's just a bit too bad that Rudolph Wharton drove your wife to the hospital."

"Why?" I asked, surprised.

Mercy shrugged elaborately. "He's a harbinger of ill-fortune."

I said, half-joking, "Now you sound like a novelist."

She narrowed her eyes at me. "It's true. Everything he touches turns to dust. My mother died in his rest home. She had a good doctor, good care, but she died nonetheless. Because of Rudolph Wharton."

"Isn't that an unreasonable statement?" I kept my voice level, I didn't want to discourage the discourse.

"It may seem so to you." She tipped the beer can, took a very long swallow. "But you don't know the man."

"Not very well," I admitted. "But he seems a pleasant enough fellow. Nothing insidious about him that I can see."

"You don't know what he did to his wife." She drank again. The can seemed to be empty.

"Let me get you another beer." I was sincerely interested in the conversation. "What did he do to his wife?" I asked returning with the refill.

"She was a Mayhew."

"A what?"

"A Mayhew. Ernestine and Eulalie Mayhew, the only daughters of Clarence Mayhew, a late and lamented gentleman who owned half the town in his day. How do you think Rudolph Wharton acquired all his property?"

"By marrying Ernestine Mayhew?"

"You are so right!" She drank from her second beer can and I wondered if she'd been tippling at home or if one should be her limit.

"How long ago was this?"

"Just about when mother and I moved here. That's —let's see—eighteen years, I think. Yes, eighteen years, all of that. She was a lady, Ernestine Mayhew, an absolute lady, but after years of living with Rudolph Wharton, that changed, I can tell you."

"Changed? In what way?"

Mercy Bird burped, said, "Excuse me. Knute, you shouldn't ask questions like that. It must be an occupational disease. I don't gossip about people."

My telephone rang. "Don't go away," I said and went to answer it. I had calls to make myself, now that I thought of it, to Gloria and Wharton, I'd promised, and Parks, I should call my partner Barry Parks and tell him about the baby, and Dennehy and my ex-partner Benedict also down in Florida . . . "Hello?"

"Knute? This is Dolly Selene."

What the devil did she want?

"Yes, Mrs. Selene?"

"Dolly, I told you . . ."

"Yes. Dolly."

"I don't want to be a pest, Knute, but I wonder if you could possibly drop by my house this evening? I'm very disturbed about something and the Wellesley police have been so rude lately when I call . . ."

It was easy to guess why the Wellesley police had been so "rude." Dolly Selene had been all over them like a wet blanket and a cop just doesn't have the time to play hand-holder for a neurotic.

"I'm sorry, Mrs. . . . Dolly. I have company now and I have to go back to the hospital to see Brenda and take her things. The baby was born today. A son."

"Oh, isn't that wonderful?" Her attempt at cheerfulness only managed to sound forlorn. She'd said that she was seriously disturbed about something. What if I turned her off and there really was something . . . ?

"Perhaps after I come back from the hospital. If it isn't too late?"

She sighed gratefully. "That would be just fine. I don't mind what time . . . it's never too late to visit a lonely old widow . . ."

I cut that off. "All right. Expect me about ten. But I won't be able to stay long."

"You're so kind. Thank you, Knute!"

Hanging up, I turned to face Mercy Bird. She was sitting with her eyes closed, looked as though she might be asleep.

"Will you have another beer?" I asked loudly.

Her eyes snapped open. "No, thank you. I must go. Give Brenda my best." She struggled to get up from the kitchen bench.

I reached out to help her, but she made it on her own. Trailing her to the door, I thanked her again. She peered out the window before opening the door. Wharton's lights were on, so were the Farleys'. What was she looking for? I wondered. As though she were afraid.

"The coast is clear," said Mercy Bird. She jerked open the door and slipped out into the night. I realized my porch lights were off, flicked them on to show the way but she was gone.

A rare bird, indeed, that Mercy. Could it be possible that she had been writing the poison-pen letters to Wharton? I didn't like to think so, but it was obviously a possibility. She blamed her mother's death on him, irrational, but motive just the same. Worth looking into, when I had time.

When I had time? Stalling, of course. I could just call the chief and give him the word. But I liked Mercy Bird. I'd hate to start off a new life in a new town by nailing a neighbor.

Why was it that life never seemed simple? Other people lived a lifetime without running into murder, robbery, arson, extortion, rape, and the rest of it. Did the crime follow the cop? Or did the cop attract the crime?

Pulling up in front of Dolly Selene's, at first I thought she'd gone to bed. The house seemed completely dark. But then I spied the shades of a colored TV, ghosts moving in a box, through the living-room window. I sighed, wished she had gone to bed, I was tired, and got out of my car, walked up the walk.

It was so dark that I couldn't see where the doorbell was so I knocked. A couple of houses down, a baby cried. Our baby would cry, all babies cried.

"Mrs. Selene. Dolly?"

The television made muted noises.

"Help," whispered the television.

The television?

"Dolly?"

"Knute? Help. Please."

I grabbed at the doorknob, turned and pulled. The door swung open. "Dolly?"

Something moved, a shifting of shadows. The thing that moved was on the floor. I went to it.

"Knute . . ." spoken through malfunctioning lips.

"What . . . where the devil is the light switch?" Kneeling, I tried to feel what was wrong, felt something sticky, felt something that felt like blood. On the head—blood.

"By . . . the . . . door."

I stood up and backtracked, felt along the sides of the door, found a switch plate. I pushed on the switch, the hall light came on, bright, too bright.

Dolly Selene, lying on the floor. Dolly Selene, dark splotches on her face and arms, bruises, blood redder than her hair. Her face contorted piteously, her mouth twisted. "He came. The telephoner. He came."

I went back to her, knelt again. Thank God, my instincts has been right. Thank God, I had agreed to come and see her, had come. I didn't do well with a guilty conscience. Delicately, I touched her hair where the blood was. She winced, began to cry.

"What happened?"

"He came to the door, spoke. I thought it was you . . ." Her voice trailed off.

"Wait. Just lie there. I'll call the station."

"I thought it was you. Come early. I was standing on the stairs, was coming down to put the lights on." I looked behind her to a staircase leading straight up. "He came in. The shape of him didn't look like you. I said, 'Who are you?' He said, 'Dr. Venable, remember me? Your friend.' I said, 'No, no, you don't,' as he came at me, there on the stairs. He grabbed me and threw me down . . ."

"Wait. Let me call. You need a doctor."

She reached for me. I noticed one of her long fingernails was broken. Even her hands looked hurt. "He heard your car. He ran—out the back."

I got up. "Where's the phone?"

"In—there." She had raised her head to speak to me, now she let it fall back, rest against the pink carpet.

I had to fumble for another light switch. A singer on the television wailed at me. There was the phone, on an end table. I dialed 235-1212.

"Wellesley Police," said a voice.

"Who's this?" I asked.

"Officer Bennotti."

"Bennotti, this is Knute Severson, Boston P.D. Send an ambulance to 11 Avon Road. There's been an assault."

"Right away."

I went back to Dolly, pulled an afghan off a sofa as I went and put it over her. "I don't want to move you," I told her. "Something might be broken. I'm going to look around. He still might be in the neighborhood." I doubted it. I was pretty damn' sure he'd taken off like a big bird, but I had to look. I spent a fruitless few minutes running around the house, peering into adjoining back yards. No sign of him, no sign at all. The neighbors, some had lights on, other houses were dark. The Wellesley boys would have to question them, now I had to see to the victim. I went back into the house. The television still blared from the other room.

I bent over Dolly and said, "They'll be here in a minute."

She began to cry again and between sobs said something I didn't catch the first time. "What?" I leaned closer.

"I must—look—terrible."

I stared at her and heard the sound of squealing brakes, turned my head to see the circling light from a cruiser just outside the house. Two figures appeared at the open door, carrying something. A stretcher. One was Dennehy.

"What's up, Knute?" He didn't wait for an answer. He and his partner began to open up the stretcher, worked quickly as though they'd done it a thousand times before. They picked Dolly up carefully, placed her on the improvised bed, moved toward the door. I followed. "Where are we going?"

"To the hospital. Come along."

"Be with you in a minute." And I stepped into the living room and turned off the TV. It went black in the middle of a commercial. I rode in the back of the station wagon cruiser, holding Dolly Selene's hand.

When they'd taken her into the emergency ward where a resident was looking her over, Dennehy introduced his partner, Officer Bly. Then, "What happened? Could she give you the story?"

I nodded. "Some of it. She said this telephone nut came calling. Attacked her on the stairs. Just before I got there, she said. I made a fast search of the grounds but no soap. Your boys may find something. My efforts were on the hit and miss side."

"What were you doing there anyway?" Bly wanted to know.

"She'd called me earlier, invited me. Said something was disturbing her. Didn't say what."

"Why didn't she call us?" was Bly's next question.

I looked at Dennehy who answered. "She's been bugging the station, especially Dorsey. Called every night almost. She's heard noises, somebody prowling, that kind of jazz. Dorsey finally told her to get off his back."

Bly grimaced. "Only this time, she wasn't fooling."

"When the doc gets through with her, maybe she can give us a description of the telephoner." Dennehy was scribbling in his notebook. "The guy's been laying off lately."

"Concentrating on Mrs. Selene, maybe," Bly suggested.

"There's the resident now," I told them. The young doctor in the white coat strode up to the emergency desk.

We descended on him. "I'm sending her to X-ray," he explained to us. "I can't find any broken bones, but better to be sure. She says somebody attacked her." He wanted to know the details, I could tell from his expression. But he wanted to play it cool, didn't intend to ask.

"Can we talk to her?" asked Dennehy.

"Well—I guess if it's necessary, for a few minutes. It'll take that long to set up the X-rays. She seems coherent enough. I'd say she acts like a woman with a lot of courage."

We said we'd take it easy on her and filed into the emergency ward. Dolly was in a curtained cubicle, staring up at the ceiling.

"You're sure it was the telephoner?" was what Dennehy wanted to know.

"Oh, yes." She tried to nod her head, gave a small gasp of pain. "I recognized his voice when he came in."

"What did he look like?"

Her eyes widened, one of them was turning black and purple underneath. "I don't really know. I didn't see him."

"You didn't see him?" asked Bly incredulously.

"It was dark, you see. I was there in the dark and he came in and said he was Venable, that's the name the telephoner had given me, that he'd come to call on me in person and I said, oh, no, and started to run up the stairs and he came after me and grabbed me . . ."

"Was he young or old? Tall or short? Surely you got some idea." Dennehy sounded impatient.

"Young, I think." She licked her lips. "Yes, I'm pretty sure. From the way he moved, like a young man. And rather tall. I think tall, taller than I anyway, he looked so big when he came at me . . . but then. Only, very strong. He was very strong." A tear rolled down from the blackened eye.

"And my arrival scared him off?" I asked her.

"Yes." She reached weakly for my hand. "Oh, thank you, Knute. Thank you for saving me."

"I'm going to have to kick you out now." The resident came up behind us. "We're going to X-ray, Mrs. Selene. And then I'll give you a sedative and you're going to get some rest. You'll feel much stronger in the morning." To us, he added, "You can take up where you left off then."

I said good night to her and we started out. I could hear her telling the young doctor she had Blue Cross-Blue Shield. The resident had diagnosed one thing very well—she did sound like a lady with a lot of guts.

Driving back to the Selene house, Bly, whom it seemed was new on the force, wanted to be filled in completely on the telephone calls. Dennehy gave him a bare rundown but I didn't listen. I was remembering when I had driven up to Dolly's house. How quiet the neighborhood had been. Just a baby crying and the faint sound of her television. Dr. Venable, whoever he was, must have been the silent type. Strange, almost impossible that I wouldn't have heard him. Once in the house, the television was louder, quite noisy, now that I thought of it. That might have covered up any sounds of hasty departure. Might have. Or, perhaps she'd been mistaken. Maybe I hadn't been the one to scare him off. It could have been the sound of some other car. It galled me to think that I could have been so close and yet missed him.

Him. Young and tall and thin. A fair enough description of Gregg Farley. Where had he been this evening, I wondered. At the hospital, Gloria had said he had the car. If he had wheels, he could have been—anywhere. I started to tell Dennehy about him, but hesitated. A Wharton-Severson hunch, a prickling of the thumbs? What was I, a cop or a mollycoddler? "What do you know about Gregg Farley?" I asked abruptly.

Dennehy stopped in mid-sentence, I hadn't realized I was interrupting him. "The kid who lives across the street from you? We've called on him and his parents a few times for one thing or another. Why? What's on your mind?"

"What kind of one thing or another?"

"Some pilfering at the high school. We couldn't hang it on him. And a sex charge. The girl was fifteen, her father wanted to tar and feather him, but it turned out that the Farley kid wasn't the only one so that fell by the wayside, too. Come on, Knute, level. You figure that Gregg Farley might be our man—or boy?"

"It wouldn't hurt to find out where he was tonight. I

haven't got anything concrete at all. In fact, I've just been wondering if it's only because I don't like the looks of him. And you know how lousy that kind of finger-pointing can be."

"Maybe so," Bly spoke wisely. "But I got a talent that way. I can look at a creep and read him clear through. And you know what, most every time it turns out that I hit the mark."

Dennehy and I exchanged glances. "We'll check the Farley kid out," he said noncommittally. He pulled up alongside my car, still standing at Dolly's curb. "I'll let you know how it turns out."

"Thanks, Dennehy." I had to squelch a yawn. "I'm going to leave you to it. I'm beat. Hey, did I tell you? Brenda had a boy today. I'm a father!"

"Yeah?" Dennehy beamed, reached into his uniform breast pocket. "Have a cigar!"

I laughed, took it. "Thanks. How come you're equipped with cigars for new fathers?"

"I had some good news tonight, too. Remember I told you I was going before the selectmen on that sergeant promotion? They finally made up their minds and, well, Knute, old boy, Detective First Grade, shake hands with Sergeant Dennehy!"

Mercy's baby gift turned out to be a pair of rather odd-looking booties made out of yellow yarn. "Isn't that nice of her," beamed Brenda, "she must have made them herself."

I held one up. "They look pretty big." I held the other one up. "Well, one of them looks pretty big."

Brenda laughed. She looked wonderful, I thought, eyes shining, hair spread against her pillow. "How soon will they let you come home?" I asked her.

"Friday, I think. I can hardly wait. Have you seen the baby today? Isn't he beautiful? He looks just like you."

"I think he looks like you." A fatuous remark, but fatherhood brought out the smug in me.

"With those big blue eyes?" Her dark eyes danced.

I leaned over and kissed her. "Like you said, he's beautiful. I've got to go now, got another sick call to make. I'll be back after dinner."

"Another sick call?"

I hadn't told her about Dolly's troubles. Didn't know how she'd take it, but . . . "Dolly Selene. They brought her in here last night. It looks as though our telephoner became an activist."

Brenda's eyes widened. "What did he do to her?"

"Roughed her up. That's why I want to drop by. To see how she is."

"Oh, dear, how terrible." She lowered her lashes. "I guess maybe I owe her an apology."

I leaned over and kissed the top of her head. "See you tonight."

"Did they catch him? The telephoner?"

"Not yet." I started for the door. I saw no need to tell her that my arrival at Dolly's may have scared him off. Quit while you're ahead, an ancient adage.

"Well, tell her I hope she's feeling better."

I nodded, gave her a goodbye smile and went down the hall. Dolly was on the fourth floor, I used the stairs. Quicker than waiting for the elevator. I had a TV dinner in the car that I'd cook for supper. Turkey. I hadn't had a TV dinner since we'd been married. Kind of looked forward to it.

Dolly Selene was sitting up in bed, wearing a frilly bed jacket that looked pretty incongruous with her lulu of a black eye.

"Knute! How nice of you to come!" She held out her hands to me and I took them, let go almost immediately.

"How are you feeling?"

She smiled bravely. "A little sore here and there, but I'm fine, I guess. The doctor says I can go home tomorrow. No broken bones. Sit down, won't you? I've been devastatingly lonesome. This is a semiprivate room but the other bed's empty and the only non-professional I've talked to all day was the volunteer who brought the newspapers."

That surprised me a little. "The police haven't been here?"

She shook her head, winced. "Nary a soul." Again the brave smile.

"Could be they're following a lead."

"Oh, I hope so. To tell you the truth, I'm a little afraid to go home." She looked at me with solemn eyes. "What if he comes back?"

"Chief Torrence will give you some protection, I'm sure. Now that you've had time to think about it, do you remember anything else?"

"That's all I've been doing, thinking." She touched the black eye with gentle fingertips. "I feel so foolish, not being able to tell you more. But it was dark and I wasn't expecting him." She sighed, the bed jacket rose to new heights, and fell. Then, eyes alert, "You say they're following a lead? They've found out something?"

"Maybe. We'll see."

She pouted. "You don't intend to tell me."

"Not yet. If it works out, you'll have to help to identify him." I couldn't tell her how tenuous a lead it was. God, how I hated the at-random criminal. They could pick on the public almost at will, it was so damned hard to catch them as long as they played it smart—and lucky.

I brought my attention back to Dolly who was saying, "With this shiner I don't know if I can do the play reading next week . . ."

"Play reading?"

"For the club I belong to, the Drama-tics. It's the last

meeting of the year and we're doing a reading of *Night Must Fall*. You don't have to pay royalties when you do a reading, you see."

"Yes. Well, you can cover the eye up with make-up or something, can't you?"

"I hope so. You're not leaving, are you? So soon?"

"I'm on my way to see Brenda," I lied. "I guess I didn't tell you—oh, yes, I did. On the telephone. The baby was born yesterday. Brenda's in the maternity ward."

"Isn't it wonderful? And how nice of you to come see me . . ." Her voice trailed off, I could have sworn she was about to add, "first." I hoped I hadn't given her any ideas. I had a hunch that Dolly Selene could take a hint better than most—and run farther with it.

"I'll check on you tomorrow," I told her, leaving.

She brightened up. "Please do. I'm going home sometime in the morning. And thanks again for coming."

"No trouble at all. I was coming to see my wife and son anyway."

I drove into the yard, half expected to find Mein waiting at the door complete with ravenous appetite, but no cat. TV dinner in hand, I walked in and set the oven, lit it to pre-heat. I went to the front door, picked the mail out of the mailbox. Two bills, four advertisements, and a letter from Benedict.

I read that while the TV cooked, at least I started to read it: *Dear Knute and Brenda, you must be settled in the new house by now. And the baby must be almost . . .*

The doorbell rang. I went out into the hall, it was dusk,

I hadn't turned the lights on but I did now, and opened the door.

A young girl in dungarees stood there, holding my cat who was struggling to get down. Delilah Farley said, "I brought your cat home."

I opened the screen door wide. "Come in. Where was he?"

"Behind our house. I was afraid he'd go on Weston Road." She released Mein who jumped down with a thump, gave her a less than grateful glare and stalked into the kitchen.

"Thank you very much." She didn't seem very anxious to leave, I glanced over at her house, no lights there either.

"I've never been in this house before." Delilah stepped past me, looked into the living room. "The Pinkhams who lived here were sourpusses. It's nice."

"Thank you."

Instead of turning back toward the door, she walked on into the living room.

"Sit down, won't you?" I said politely. "Can I get you a Coke or something?"

"No, thanks." The no thanks must have been for the Coke because she did sit on the Boston rocker that Brenda'd brought from her father's manse in New Hampshire. She sat gingerly, tested its rockers, settled back some and glanced airily around the room.

Mein came to the hall archway and meowed.

Delilah looked at the cat, looked away.

"Do you like cats?" I asked, not giving a damn whether

she did or didn't. What do you say to a teen-age girl who just sits there staring?

"Not especially." She began, slowly, to rock. She laced her fingers together, watched them as she began to rotate her thumbs.

Mein repeated his request.

"Will you excuse me a moment while I go feed him?" Something told me I'd better check the TV dinner, too.

"Sure." She didn't even look up.

I put food in Mein's dish, decided the turkey was done and turned the oven off. When I returned, she was still sitting there, rocking.

"Something on your mind, Delilah?"

She shrugged elaborately.

"I can't react to it, whatever it is, if you won't tell me."

"I guess not."

"Well?"

"Yes, you've got a nice house here."

"We like it."

"My mother says you work in Boston, right?"

"That's right. I'm a detective with the Boston Police Department. District One."

"Yeah. That's what she said."

I didn't know what to say next so I waited. She got up, went to the window and looked out toward her house. Then she turned and found a new place to sit, in the wing chair.

"The fuzz—the Wellesley cops—police have got my brother down at the station. That's where my mother and father are, too."

"What for?"

"For nothing. Just because he's bugged them a couple of times. Because he's got long hair. And Gregg says how he wears his hair is his own business. He told them that already and he told me he was really going to lay it on them if they laid it on him. Just because of his hair."

"What is it they say he did?"

She made a face. If she'd comb her hair back and wear something feminine, she'd have been a nice-looking girl, I thought. "They don't say he did anything. They say"—and she changed her voice to mimic authority—"we just want to ask you some questions, Farley. About telephones, Farley. Just a few questions about telephones."

"And they asked your mother and father to come down, too?"

"Yep. They call it protecting his rights." She flung her head back so the hair came out of her eyes and she could look directly at me. "I eavesdropped when they were at the house. They think Gregg's been making dirty phone calls. And he hasn't. I could tell them he hasn't, but they wouldn't listen to me."

"How do you know he hasn't?"

"Because he's my brother, that's how! For God sakes, I've lived with him all my life, I ought to know. And some kids I know don't like their brothers and sisters, but Gregg and I, we always got along just fine. So I know him. Better'n anybody." Her eyes blazed. They were gray eyes. Rather pretty.

"Unfortunately, we've got to have more than that to go on, we cops. As we go along being cops, we run into all kinds of people whose families tell us, 'but he's a good boy—or he's a good man.' Only sometimes, they're wrong.

So we get what you might call suspicious." I didn't know what she wanted from me, but I was damned hungry and wished she'd get to it.

"Oh, I know. I'm not stupid, you know. I know that the cops are down on Gregg because he's done a couple of little things. Nothing big, just little. Like he spray-painted some street signs once with a big peace symbol. They made him clean 'em all off and paint the signs again. And even after he'd done it, and done it good, they were still down on him. So once"—she smiled at the thought of it—"he squirted a water pistol right in Sergeant Dorsey's face! Boy, was he mad."

"That's because Gregg showed a lack of respect for authority." God, I thought, I must be getting old. I sounded like a prissy old schoolteacher I'd had at BC High.

"Jesus, don't be so patronizing!" Delilah Farley jumped up and started for the door.

"Hold it, will you?" I went after her. "I'm sorry. You're trying to explain something to me and I want to listen. Come back and sit down. You were saying Gregg did a couple of little things . . . dropping out of school, though. That's not so little."

She didn't retrace her steps but stood in the doorway. "There's no law against it! He just got fed up. Nothing mattered. How could anything matter when you come from such . . ." She licked her lips, she was getting to the hard part and I thought "here it comes" but she backed off. "For a while, it got better. When Mrs. Wharton was around. He could go over and talk to her, she'd listen." Her lips curled. "But then, they broke that up."

"Who broke that up?" I'd have to let her tell it her way, I could see that.

"My folks, of course. People with dirty minds. My father said Gregg had no business spending so much time alone with a married woman and my mother said, 'Gregg, it really doesn't look good, you're almost a grown man now . . .' Jesus, it made me want to throw up! Gregg did throw up. I heard him when they were done, upstairs in the bathroom."

I frowned. Smoke equals fire? The letters threatening Wharton—could there be a tie-in? Little did Delilah Farley know that I was as mistrustful of her brother as anyone. And why, really? Long hair didn't light my fire, but it didn't turn me off either. Only, every so often Gregg Farley's name would fit into a corner of the puzzles. But which puzzle? Or, neither? A piece from another jigsaw entirely?

"What do they do to someone who makes dirty phone calls?" Delilah wanted to know.

"It depends. Often, it means psychiatric treatment . . ."

"The state nut house?"

"State institutions are prepared to deal . . ."

"How do they catch someone like that? Put bugs on the phones, stuff like that? Last year some kids were calling the high school, saying there was a bomb. They said then they had the school phone bugged and the kid, or kids just called other places. Once they called my mother's office and told the newspaper and the newspaper had to call the school. There wasn't any bomb, but my mother said they couldn't take chances. Finally, they stopped letting us out at school and the phone calls stopped. Not much fun to just walk outside while they look inside and then have to go back anyway."

"Well, yes, they try to trace the calls." I wasn't about to tell her that was sometimes impossible. "The best way to catch an obscene phone caller is to catch him calling—or lure him someplace. Get him to show his face so he can be identified."

She thought about that. "Well, anyway, Gregg didn't do it and they can't prove he did, can they?"

"Not if he didn't." Apparently the Wellesley police hadn't mentioned Dolly's attack in Delilah's presence so I tried a gambit. "Where was your brother last night?"

"Out."

"Out where?"

"Down at the Youth Center awhile, I guess. Just out. Anywhere he wanted to be. Why?" Eyes narrowed.

"If you know where he was, someplace where it could be proven, you could get him off the hook. That's all."

"Yeah?" Her face brightened. "Soon as he comes home, I'll ask him. Where he was. Every minute."

"I'd guess that the police have already done the asking. Maybe when he comes home, he'll be clear."

She doubted it. I could tell by her face. "Maybe." A shake of the hair. "How I wish we could go away, Gregg and I! To someplace where nobody knows us."

"You can one day when you're old enough."

"Old enough!" She almost spat the words. It was easy to imagine she'd heard them a million times. "That's what they always say." Again the change of tone. "Delilah, dear, you aren't old enough!"

I made a stab at it. "Any special reason why you and Gregg hate your folks so much?"

An oblique glance, more lip licking, then, "Sure. Sure there is. Wouldn't you hate your folks, too, if they were lousy, dirty wife-swappers?"

I felt my mouth drop. This, I hadn't expected. "Your mother? And father?"

"Who else?" She put on that closed young mask that so many kids wear for self-protection. "You know that bunch of beauts that was over at the house the other night when you were there? Well, they all play the game. It's group therapy, or something, for them. Gregg and I found it out one night by accident and after that"—she shrugged—"nothing mattered."

"Which was when Gregg dropped out of school?"

"Yep. I would have, too, but damn it, I like school. And I want to go to college. I wouldn't give it up, not for them. I told Gregg he was a fink and he just said maybe one day he'd have the guts to kick the old man in the . . ." She stopped, decided to finish with, "In the tail and get the hell out."

Lights flashed on across the street and I said, "I think they're back. What do you want me to do?"

"Put in a good word for Gregg, they should listen to you. Tell them about them, if you want to. But make the fuzz listen, make them believe he couldn't have been making those dirty phone calls."

"I'll see what I can do." And maybe I would, at that. A young man so moral that the discovery of his parents' promiscuity would throw him completely off base . . . but, off base enough to whisper dirty words from the anonymity of a phone booth? How far was off base, any-way? And Delilah Farley, what hid behind that disheveled head of hair besides a pair of sharp gray eyes?

Digging into my luke-warm somewhat dried-out turkey dinner, I thought, Wife-swapping. Well, well, what do you know?

I was drinking a beer and reading the *Townsman*, the local newspaper, and Brenda was sitting at the desk, doing something with a pencil and paper. The baby, bless his heart, had had his supper and gone to bed.

"Knute," Brenda spoke thoughtfully, "what do you think of the second Sunday in July?"

They had appointed eight new policemen to the Wellesley force, I was just reading about it, so I said, "As Sundays go, I'd say it could hold its own."

"Silly! Pay attention, please. I mean, for the christening."

I took the paper away from my face and said, "The christening?"

"Well, yes. Of course. My father will come down and do it and you can invite the people from Division One and we'll ask the neighbors, naturally, and your friend Dennehy and his girl and who else shall we ask? I'm making a list."

"So many people? Listen, Brenda, I hadn't even thought about a christening. I mean, we aren't exactly churchy."

"I know we aren't, but we're going to be." She swung around to face me. "Leif is going to have the same solid religious background we had."

"You had."

"You, too. Pooh-pooh it if you like, and I'll admit being a minister's daughter sent me off the deep end at times, but Leif has to go to Sunday school and learn all those Bible stories and find the security that a firm belief can bring." Her chin shot up and I knew she meant it. Yes, indeed, she meant it.

"There go my Sundays," I muttered, the tag line of an old joke but maybe she didn't know the joke which was just as well because she ignored my remark.

"Is the second Sunday in July all right with you then?" she insisted.

"Some people will be on vacation," I demurred.

"That can't be helped. I don't want to wait until September." She swung back to the desk, every line of her back spelling determination.

I finished my article and turned the page of the paper. I was looking for the police notes, I always got a charge out of them, they seemed to run to stolen bicycles and minor accidents for the most part and from my point of view that was refreshing.

An article on the third page caught my eye. I scanned it and asked, "Hey, how'd you like to go to a play reading Friday night?"

"A what?" She wasn't concentrating on me.

"A play reading. There's a little theater group called the Drama-tics and they're doing *Night Must Fall*. Your friends, the Farleys, are in it."

"And your friend Dolly Selene?"

I looked up innocently. "Is she? I guess she is." I grinned. "Don't tell me you're getting jealous again?"

"Of that woman? Of course not. But I can't go and leave the baby."

"There are such things as baby sitters. I think I saw some ads in the classifieds."

"He's too young to leave yet." She gave me a sidewise look. "If you're going, you'll have to go alone."

I shook the paper, folded to the police notes. "Maybe I will."

There was a moment's silence.

"Knute."

"Umm?"

"You're not just interested in a play reading, are you? You've got something else on your mind."

"Could be."

"Gloria told me the police had had Gregg in to question him on that telephone business. Did you know that?"

"Uh-huh."

"They let him go home, but she thinks they're still watching him."

"Perhaps they are."

"Knute—look at me! I'm quite fond of Gloria Farley, she's been very nice to me. Do you think her son is involved in that nasty business?"

I leveled with her. "He could be."

"He could be? A boy, that's all he is, a boy. How could he be?"

"I don't have any positive arguments to give you, Madam Legal Eagle. Those years as a legal secretary really channeled your thinking. I just say, he could be. Little things—just call it a hunch, a maybe."

"A maybe-hunch?" She pursed her mouth. "You know what you are? A bulldog. The perfect police mentality. Once you get hold of a piece of something, just a little tiny piece, you never let go. You hold it in reserve, letting it grow like mushrooms in the dark, and sooner or later you'll add this little bit to it and that little bit and then —you'll pounce . . ."

I put down the paper. "Brenda"—an attempt at humor, a weak attempt—"you're mixing your metaphors. Bulldogs don't pounce, cats do."

"Oh, Knute." Her eyes grew bright, tears, I thought, could be near. "I'm a live-and-let-live person. This quality in you—it's the one thing that disturbs me. You're always so suspicious. Of everybody."

I needed the most positive, concise statement I could make. The "one thing" as she put it was what made Knute Severson run and I didn't care for the term suspicious. "I'm not vindictive, Brenda, and I don't go around thinking, aha, I wonder what he's up to under that façade. It's just that—little unsolved crimes lead to big crimes, again often unsolved." Her expression irritated me. "All right, so that's oversimplification. And generalization. I'm a simple-minded, general sort of man."

"But Gloria Farley is a friend . . . and unless you have something substantial, to persecute the boy . . ."

"Damn it, Brenda, I'm not persecuting anybody. I see nothing so awful about answering questions, clearing the air. Just one look at that kid and anybody can tell something's bothering him. Maybe a little respect for law and order will . . ."

"Oh, Knute Severson, you're impossible." By God she meant it.

Young Leif whimpered upstairs.

We glared at each other.

"Your baby is crying." I looked up the stairway. He whimpered again.

"When he cries, he's my baby. When you're bragging to your friends, he's your baby, or, at best, our baby."

"Sorry," I said coldly. "Our baby is crying." And when she had gone up to him, I didn't know whether to feel guilty because I'd lost my temper or affronted because she'd shown a considerable lack of understanding. What was she so burned up about anyway? All I'd done was tell Dennehy he could do well to check into the Farley kid's whereabouts the night Dolly was attacked. Apparently, he was clean. All well and good. What did Brenda expect me to do—lay back when friends or relatives might be involved? She knew me better than that.

She must have figured it out for herself, how unreasonable she'd been, because when she came down she apologized. "I'm sorry, Knute. Gloria was over today, all upset about the boy. He seems to be quite a handful and I guess she just got me worked up, too."

"Forget it, I will. What was ailing young Leif?" I hadn't said anything about Delilah Farley's visit and this was not the time to go into any of that. Besides, I wasn't sure I bought her story. My police mentality, as Brenda called it, required a certain amount of proof whether my wife thought so or not.

"Just a wet diaper. At least I think that's all it was. God knows I'm no expert. He went back to sleep, bless his little heart, as soon as I changed him." She brushed a loose lock of hair out of her eyes. "I think I'll go to bed myself. These two o'clock feedings wear me out."

"I know what you mean. How much longer does this go on?"

"He'll sleep through the night when he's around six weeks old, Dr. Abraham says." She went to the front door and called Mein. Standing there, waiting for him, she commented, "I think the rascal has been catching squirrels again. I smell something funny out in the front yard. There's probably a corpse in the rhododendron bush."

"Oh? I'll give it a look in the morning if you'll remind me. Don't wait if he won't come. I'll get him in before I come up."

"All right." She came away from the door, stepped on the bottom step, hesitated. "I almost forgot. Mr. Wharton is coming to dinner Saturday night."

"Wharton? How come?"

"He was so nice the day I went to the hospital, I felt I should do something. And besides, I feel sorry for the man. He's so lonely. When I invited him, he seemed so pleased. It's sad, you know. I don't think he has many friends."

I knew better than to say what I was thinking. Wharton. Damn. I didn't like the man much. No particular reason. Not one that I'd been able to figure out. When I did try to figure it out. Which wasn't often.

"Good night, darling." She was going on up. "Don't stay down here too long. You need your sleep, too."

"I'll be along as soon as I finish this brew." Which was a fib because I had another can before Mein finally answered my call and deigned to appear at the front door. I look over at Wharton's house. Small light in the upstairs bedroom. Shadowy window. Was somebody standing there looking out? Seemed so. Looking out at what? At me, at my house?

No, I didn't know why it was, but Rudolph Wharton made my nose twitch. Which reminded me. I said to Mein, "Have you been turning the rhodie bush into a squirrel graveyard?"

He looked up at me with guileless eyes. Who? Me?

They were all there at the Drama-tics play reading. Arlen and Gloria, Dolly, Christopher and Christine Beal and Harvey and Angela Klett and some three dozen others.

Arlen and Dolly were members of the cast. Arlen played Danny, the bellboy who carried the woman's head in the hatbox, and Dolly was Mrs. Bramson, the old lady Danny was out to murder. They were both pretty good. Her black eye hardly showed at all.

"Knute, how nice of you to come!" Dolly grabbed both my hands and squeezed them.

"Didn't know you dig the theater." Arlen showed all his pretty teeth in a wide smile. His slang phrases struck me as slightly off key, made me think the man was trying too hard to be with it.

"I enjoyed the play very much," I told them.

"Ever do any acting yourself?" asked a willowy brunette who'd been introduced to me as Margot Kennicut.

"No. Never. For me, it's a spectator sport."

"Too bad," she purred. "You're a great leading man type."

"Listen," Dolly plucked at my sleeve, "I've asked some people back to the house for a drink. You'll come, won't you?"

"I guess I can. Sure."

"Where's Brenda?" asked Gloria Farley, joining our circle.

"She didn't want to leave the baby just yet," I told her.

Gloria smiled knowingly. "She'll get over that." I thought she looked more washed out than usual. As though something was eating just below the surface. Brenda had said she was worried about the boy. That was probably the reason.

"If you don't act, I'll bet you'd be great at scenery building, painting," Margot Kennicut was insisting.

"As a handy man, I'm a wash out. Ask my wife."

Margot pouted. "I think he doth protest too much."

"Oh, we'll get him to join, don't worry." Arlen spoke heartily, threw his arm around Margot as he did so and gave her a very friendly hug. More than friendly?

"Are we ready?" Dolly looked around. "I'll start now and meet you at the house."

"Get going then." Arlen slapped her playfully on the rear. "My tongue is hanging out."

"Want to go in my car?" Margot asked me.

"No, thanks. I know where it is."

I thought she gave me a quick look. "Okay. You're on your own."

Dolly's living room, properly lit, proved to be a variation on a theme, all in shades of pink. I hadn't even noticed when I was there before, had my mind on things other than décor. I wondered how the late Robert Selene had felt about pink carpeting, hot pink curtains, seashell pink sofa, even pink, painted brick fireplace. About the only thing that wasn't pink was the television and I guessed they didn't make them in that color. Otherwise, she would have had one.

Arlen offered to do the bartending chores in the kitchen and a good part of the assemblage went with him so I had a chance to cut Gloria out from the small herd that remained for some conversation. After a general lead-in, I got to the point. "Delilah was over to see me the other day."

"Delilah?" She should wear a brighter lipstick, I decided. She needed more color in her face.

"She was concerned about her brother."

"Was she?" She lowered almost colorless lashes. "They've always been very close." Spoken almost bitterly.

"I don't mean to be butting in, but Brenda tells me you've been worried about the boy."

"Worried!" She laughed sharply. "I guess you could say that. What do you do with a child that's gone—or is rapidly going from bad to worse? Who won't listen to you, doesn't even hear you? You can't throw up your hands, toss him in the trash barrel and get a new model."

"Have you thought of psychological counseling?"

"Arlen won't hear of it. Arlen is from the school of 'I sowed my wild oats and look how well I turned out.' The boy, says Arlen, will outgrow it." Her mouth tightened, an unspoken opinion of her husband's theory.

"What's the big problem? Drugs? Girls? Can you pin it down?"

"I don't think drugs. He swears not and I don't see how

he could be . . . I should say, he swears not when he talks to me. Which is not often. I get a lot of the silent treatment."

"What about girls?"

She shook her head. "I almost wish it were. Maybe I could cope with that. He just goes off—runs might be a better word for it. I don't know where he is most of the time. And if I don't let him take my car, he goes off on that motorbike or with one of his pals and frankly, I worry about that even more. Some of them are such reckless drivers, that Turk has been in two accidents and he's only nineteen. I think Gregg is a pretty good driver, I worry less when he has his own transportation." She looked at me almost shyly. "I suppose you think I'm one of those overindulgent mothers."

"Come and get it," bawled Arlen from the kitchen. "This operation is strictly cash and carry."

"Delilah said the police had him in for questioning." I wondered if she'd level with me. Or if she'd guessed that I already knew about it.

"Oh, yes." The brittle laugh came. "They got the idea that he might be making these obscene phone calls." Her eyes grew suddenly damp. "How do you think it feels to be the mother of a suspected obscene phone caller?"

"But he wasn't?"

"How do I know? How do I know anything? He said he didn't do it. They couldn't prove he did. But a boy that strikes his father, swears at his mother, takes money from her purse—how do I know what he's capable of? Or incapable of?"

She'd told me the truth, I had to return the favor. Not a pleasant duty, but I felt I must. It might—just might— help.

"Delilah says she knows what's in back of his miserable attitude."

"Delilah knows!" Her face flushed, oddly enough becoming more attractive in her anger. "You see? That's what's wrong with this family. Secrets. Everybody has secrets."

"She says he found out his parents played the wife-swapping game." I said it gently, softly so that no one could hear even though there was little danger of it. They were all out in the kitchen now.

"She says—what?" The new color went, left her face ashen.

"What are you two doing holding a tête-à-tête out here?" Dolly came through from the kitchen, carrying a tray with glasses. "It isn't fair, Gloria, to monopolize the most attractive man around."

Gloria looked away, didn't answer. Right then I could have given Dolly Selene a second black eye. Damn the woman! "We were just discussing the results of the last election," I answered lightly. Who said I couldn't act?

"How dreadfully dull. Here's your drink, Knute. Scotch and soda if I remember correctly. And another for Gloria."

A burst of laughter came from the kitchen. "Arlen's telling stories," Dolly said, sitting on the other side of me. "Nobody tells dirty stories as well as Arlen."

Gloria, face still averted, reached for her glass, took a long drink from it. Margot Kennicut now joined us. "What are you people doing out here when the party's going on in there?" Margot sat on a pink brocade chair that might have belonged in a boudoir, and showed a lot of leg. "Tell me about yourself, Knute Severson. I have an obligation to ask, being a divorcée. You never find gold if you don't pan for it."

Gloria stood up. "Excuse me. May I use your powder room, Dolly?"

"Certainly. You know where it is, don't you?"

"Yes, I remember." And she left without looking at anybody.

"I don't think Gloria looks well, do you?" Margot asked Dolly.

"No, I don't. And I'm not talking behind her back. I told her tonight that she should have a checkup."

"Speaking of checkups, Dolly," I interjected, "how are you feeling after your experience?"

She smiled gratefully at me. "Oh, I'm fine, honestly. It seems so long ago, almost as though it never happened. Chief Torrence called to say he'd have to call off his surveillance, he's short of men and I told him I understood." Her smile turned brave. "I can't spend the rest of my life being afraid of every shadow, can I? Besides, I'm sure he won't be back."

"You're sure?" Margot's tone was odd. "How can you be sure?"

Dolly shrugged. The dress she wore was a multicolored print cut low in front and when she shrugged interesting things happened if one looked closely. "I just feel it. I just think he must know I have police protection and he won't come back."

"I hope you're right," I told her.

She batted her eyelashes at me. "If I have any trouble, I know who to call. My knight errant, Knute Severson."

Margot tittered. "The modern-day Sir Galahad."

I drank the rest of my drink. Gloria hadn't returned and I was pretty sure that when she did, I was not about to have another chance to talk privately. "I'd better be going along."

"So soon?" Dolly made a moue.

"It's early." Margot widened her green eyes at me.

"Maybe so, but my wife and I have a new baby who loves to get us up in the middle of the night."

"Wife? New baby?" Margot sighed dramatically. "Damn. Just my luck."

"Even so, you wouldn't have a chance, Margot, dear," Dolly smiled sweetly. "I saw him first."

"But, Dolly, love, don't be piggy. You have your obscene telephone man." And I saw that Margot's eyes looked just like Mein's when he'd done something particularly horrendous.

I left the ladies, claws bared and fur ruffled.

Saturday was one of those days.

Early on, Central Complaint gave Parks and me the job of assisting an ambulance crew in handling "a violent woman." The ambulance was on its way to Boston City Hospital and the woman passenger went berserk on route, pulled a pair of scissors out of her handbag and went for one of the attendants. The attendant behind the wheel stopped the vehicle on Storrow Drive and yelled to passers-by to call the police. Central Complaint, alias the Turret, got twelve phone calls within minutes of each other reporting the same incident which was some kind of evidence that the so-called public apathy isn't quite as apathetic as pictured.

The "violent woman" and the threatened attendant were in the ambulance when we got there. The driver was outside, waving cars past and a fair-to-middling traffic jam was developing. We used the siren to get through and instead of the ambulance driver being grateful, he glared at us when we came up to him and hissed, "You damn' fools! You want her to cut him open when she hears all that racket? She's got him pinned with a pair of shears at his throat and she's as crazy as a loon. You idiots!"

Parks took the rear door and I went in through the front. We moved simultaneously, we'd worked together long enough now so that we didn't have to plan it, we just did it.

"Hold it, lady," said Parks calmly, and I pointed my gun as he did, said, "We're police officers. Put down those scissors."

I was the closest to her. The attendant backed against the inner wall of the ambulance was a black man and he was sweating bullets. The woman, God, she looked about my mother's age and had a head of gray hair set carefully in sculptured waves, was literally drooling and her eyes were wild.

"Sons of bitches, sons of bitches," she screamed and jabbed with the scissors. At the same moment, I pushed the attendant to one side and grabbed her scissor hand. Grabbed the scissors might be a better description. She got me in the hand with them, but by that time Parks had her from the rear and I'd got the scissors.

The "violent woman" crumpled in Parks's rough embrace and burst into tears. Between the sobs I could make out a few words ". . . after me . . . out to get me . . . out to put me away."

The driver slid in beside me, breathing hard. "Jesus," he panted.

"You can say that again," his buddy put in, managing a weak smile.

"Put the restraints on her," ordered the driver.

"Here, I'll give you a hand." Parks and the black attendant laced her down with comparative ease. All she did was cry hopelessly and murmur, "Put me away."

"Thanks, man." The driver turned on his ignition. "Hey" —he gave me a second look—"you're bleeding."

I pulled out my handkerchief and tied it around my hand. Damn, blood on my best blue suit. "I'd better ride along with you," I told him. "Parks, tell Captain Granger I'll be back as soon as I can."

He looked in at me. "Is it bad?"

"I don't think so. Just a puncture, but it's messy."

"I'll follow and call in from the hospital." He looked out the windshield. "The uniformed boys are here, they've got traffic moving."

"Okay. Come on, boys, let's go. This is my new Sunday go to meeting suit and on a cop's pay I can't afford another one."

It was only a puncture but I knew it would throb like hell come night and it took over an hour to go through all the red tape and get it fixed up and that was only the beginning of that Saturday.

A little before 3 P.M., Parks and I drove to an auto dealer's on Commonwealth Avenue. Mickey Urey, the dealer, had called in the State Police when a man, "just a kid, actually," brought in a 1970 El Dorado for resale. He'd given Urey's salesman a registration slip made out to Harold Rooney with a Joy Street address. The salesman made an offer, the "kid" accepted and the salesman brought Urey the papers to cinch the deal. Urey, looking out through his office window at the seller, became suspicious and told the salesman to stall. "Ask him if he'd rather have cash than a check," Urey suggested.

The salesman returned with a yes answer. "Then tell him to come back this afternoon, we don't keep that much on hand but we'll get it by the end of the day." And as soon as the young man left, Urey called the State boys.

The registration checked. The car did belong to Harold Rooney and we were sent to check on same. Harold Rooney wasn't home but his wife was. She was aged maybe forty or forty-five and her husband, who was a manufacturer's representative, had gone out to Honeywell Data Processing to tout his product.

"Honeywell in Wellesley?" I asked.

"Yes, he had a luncheon appointment with the purchasing agent."

"Can you reach him on the phone?"

She would try, she said. And she did, and Harold Rooney went out to the parking lot and found his 1970 El Dorado missing. Which is why we went to Mickey Urey's. The kid hadn't come back for his money yet, maybe he wouldn't, maybe he'd been scared off, but we were going to hang around just in case.

"The new Caddies don't look like fancy tanks any more," Parks commented as we looked around the showroom, posing as potential buyers.

"No question they're a fine car," I agreed. "A lot of money, but they last forever. My father has a friend up in New Hampshire who's still driving a '51. Or, he was when I last heard. Runs like a watch, my dad says." I moved my left arm, held the left wrist by the right hand, pulled it in close to my body.

"Is it bothering you?" asked Parks.

"Some. I'll be okay. Shift's nearly over anyway and I've got two days coming."

"You'd better take good care of it. Those puncture wounds can be dangerous."

"They gave me a tetanus shot. Maybe that's why I feel kind of dopey."

There was a tapping on glass behind us and I turned to see Mickey Urey mouthing words from behind his office window. We went over to see what he wanted.

"I'm about to knock off," he told us. "My wife's expecting me down at the Cape, she thinks it's bad enough that I have to come in on Saturdays, but if I'm not there by 6 or 6:30, she blows a gasket."

I looked at my watch. Almost five. "When do you close?"

"Six o'clock."

"The salesman, Danny Crater, is it? Can he hang around to identify the guy if he shows up?"

"Sure. Why don't you take a seat and I'll send Danny in. If the kid comes, he'll have to ask for Danny anyway. That's the way we left it."

Danny Crater had sleek dark hair, a little long in back, and muttonchop sideburns. "It's been a rough day," he told us conversationally. "I had two possibles but no sale and then this punk trying to sell a hot car. This is some business, I'll tell you. Sometimes I don't know why I've put fifteen years into it."

I could have told him that our business had its minuses, too, but I didn't get the chance because one of the other salesmen stuck his head in the door and said, "Hey, Danny, there's a Rooney here to see you."

I had my back to the window and I turned casually to get a look at Mr. Rooney, uncertain whether it would be the real Mr. Rooney or the pretender.

I looked straight into the eyes of Gregg Farley. We stared at each other for at least a full minute and then he bolted.

Parks and I went after him. He ran past the shiny Cadillacs in the showroom, out into the used car lot, dodged between the rows of "creampuffs" with the two of us racing after.

I caught up with him and he swung. I swung back with my left hand, damn, and connected. I nearly passed out with the pain but Gregg Farley went down and Parks grabbed him while I leaned against a hood and fought nausea.

The car had been stolen in Wellesley. And he was from Wellesley, he was Wellesley's baby. We informed him of his rights and put him on ice until somebody could come in for him. Chief Torrence, on the telephone said, "Isn't he a neighbor of yours?"

"Yeah," I told him. "Break it gently to his mother, will you? It'll throw her."

And I went back to see if I couldn't do something for the kid, but the little jerk wouldn't even open his mouth except to say, "Ever since you came, everything's lousy."

And still, the day wasn't over.

I got home finally and it was close to seven. It was late, my hand hurt and Wharton was due at 7:30. I'd hardly set foot in the door when Brenda informed me, "Knute, the most awful thing happened today. That obscene telephone caller—he called here!"

I stared at her. "But our number isn't in the book."

"I know." She looked pale. It had shaken her.

"Then, how . . . how could he know about us, we're so new here. Did he call you by name?"

"Yes."

"What time was this?"

"I was fixing Leif's formula . . . it must have been about 5:30."

About 5:30. Later than his usual hour . . . 5:30. It was 5:30 or so when Gregg Farley showed up to collect his ill-gotten gains. But it had to be someone who knew us then—or at least knew of us. It had to be.

"Knute, I didn't even notice . . . what's the matter with your hand?"

"I nicked it. Don't worry, it's okay. This guy who called, what did he say? What did he sound like?"

"It was the way Dolly Selene said. I listened more than I wanted to because I thought you'd want to know." She touched my bandaged hand gently, shuddered at the memory. "It was awful. Such filth."

"But you couldn't recognize the voice?"

"No, but that's the one thing that was different. Dolly said, I think Dolly said, that he had a deep voice. Sexy, she called it. This wasn't. It was—distorted. I wondered if he were speaking through something that muffled it. He sounded so far away."

"Damn," I said. "I wish I'd been here!" But I wasn't, of course, and he must have known that. Only, how? Two rules he'd broken, he'd called after four and on a Saturday. He had to know I'd be away. That was for sure.

"Come on, darling," Brenda drew me toward the living room. "I'll give you a Scotch. Rudolph Wharton will be here in a few minutes. We'll talk about it later."

"Is the baby in bed?"

"Yes. Asleep, I hope." We went into the kitchen where Mein was concentrating on a dish of food. I rubbed his back which he arched as he purred through a mouthful.

"I've got news for you, too," I said as Brenda fixed my drink. "You're not going to like it, but we arrested Gregg Farley this afternoon."

"Oh, Knute!" She dropped an ice cube which slithered across the floor. Mein eyed it, decided his dish was more interesting.

I told her how it happened and she shook her head mournfully. "Poor Gloria," she sighed.

"Aren't you having a drink?" I asked. Mine tasted good, damn' good. I just might survive.

"Yes, in a minute. I've got to check the chicken breasts in the oven. What will happen to the boy?"

"He's over seventeen, no juvenile. But he's not twenty-one either. It depends. First offense, he might get proba-tion." I let my voice go bitter. "Might, hell. Most of 'em do on first offense. Which is half our problem."

The doorbell rang.

"That must be Wharton," I said. "I'll go."

It was Mercy Bird wearing a red and green kilt skirt, a purple sweater and a tam-o'-shanter pulled over all her hair. She was carrying something, as usual. This time it was a book. "My latest," she said, thrusting it into my good hand. "An advance copy. What did you do to your other hand?"

"Scratched it." I looked at the cover of the book, read the title, *The Foo Dog*. "Thanks," I said, "won't you come in?"

"Another time," she told me. "You're having company." I glanced across the street, Rudolph Wharton was coming out of his front door.

"Well, yes, but . . ."

"Another time." And she took off, all flashing colors, a garish rainbow.

I found Wharton hard to talk to. Brenda didn't, thank goodness. Which left me time to drink my drinks and think about the thorn in my side, the obscene phone caller. He'd made it personal now and that burned me. Which led me to ask Wharton, during a lull in the conversation, "Have you received any more of those letters?"

He looked a little startled, I thought; well, I had changed the subject somewhat abruptly. "No, I haven't," he told me.

"Letters?" asked Brenda. Then, understanding, she looked embarrassed. As though I'd done something rude or lewd or something.

"Strange that he'd just stop—like that," I said thoughtfully.

"Yes, I suppose it is, but God knows I'm grateful. You tell yourself to pay no attention, but just the same it gets to you. The thought that someone could hate me that much." He smiled his bright smile. "I didn't think I was that much of a louse."

"I guess men in the public eye pick up their share of animosity," I philosophized.

He nodded. "Oh, that's true enough. Can't be helped. Can't please all of the people all of the time. But that kind of venom—I just can't conceive it. If I were just an ordinary citizen, he could have done me a great deal of harm. You know how rumors are, they make people mistrustful. Human nature."

I raised my eyebrows. "But when a rumor is untrue, blatantly untrue . . . what actual damage could that sort of lie do? It seems to me, the effect might be the opposite. A says that B did C. The authorities investigate, prove that B did not commit C. Therefore, B gets the sympathy, A gets the resentment, perhaps even the blame. You see what I mean?"

"I hadn't thought of it that way, but yes, I do. I suppose in the long run it might work out that way." He sighed. "I certainly hope so. I could stand a little sympathetic treatment."

"Well, I think A is an absolutely dreadful individual," said Brenda firmly. "Come on, you two. It's time to eat."

Over dinner, thank God I'd hurt my left hand, I could manage with my right and I was starving, I told them about my visit to the Drama-tics the night before. "Ever been to any of those things?" I asked Wharton. "They seem to be pretty professional at it. If you like plays."

"My wife and I went a time or two." He turned to my wife. "You are a talented cook, Brenda. This chicken is excellent."

"Thank you. Will you have some more wine?" She

looked especially lovely tonight, I observed. Could be the candlelight.

"I'll have some." I offered my glass. "That Dolly Selene is a very good actress. I wonder if she was ever a professional."

"A professional what?" asked Brenda under her breath.

Wharton didn't hear her. "I wouldn't know. I don't know the Selenes that well." He sipped from his refilled wineglass. "What kind of white wine is this?"

"Do you like it?" Brenda looked pleased. "It's a sauterne. You don't think it's too dry? Knute thinks it's a little too dry."

"I think it's perfect." And he toasted her with it.

I believe that's when I decided that I wanted to know more about Ernestine Mayhew Wharton. Why any woman would walk out on this masculine paragon was something of a mystery.

The Town Clerk's office was in the Town Hall and the Town Hall was a red stone castle on top of a hill. It didn't have a moat but it had a duck pond where a group of mothers with little kids were busily feeding the fowl. I made a note to remember to tell Brenda to bring Leif there when he got a little bigger. There were geese, ducks, even swans, and the atmosphere was bucolic.

The Town Clerk was a Mrs. Davis who must have been trained in the old school because unlike some Town Clerks I'd met, she was gracious, courteous, and patient.

I had a cover story, made it up in bed the night before when I decided that Rudolph Wharton might just learn that I was looking up his wife's history. "I'm trying to trace a family that lived here maybe twenty years ago," I told the Town Clerk after telling her my name. "My mother, she lives in Florida, had these relatives, you see, and she's lost track of them. So the bad thing is that I'm not certain of the spelling of the name. It was Marz or Mars or March, maybe even Marche, she's not sure. They weren't close relatives, you see, but . . ."

"Oh, my," laughed Mrs. Davis. "Isn't it strange how vague family ties can be? I suppose you'd like to look through our residents' listings . . . M-A, did you say? You're certain of that much? M-A something?"

"Yes." I gave her my best smile. "That much I'm sure of."

"Well, come with me. But you must put them back in order, you know. Filed alphabetically, just so. It would be terrible if we lost one of our listings or if it got out of place."

"I'll be very careful. I promise."

She started me in the M-A file drawer, watched for a few minutes to see how carefully I handled her precious listings and then went off. I flipped to MAYHEW, Ernestine Matilda.

The card contained a mini-history. Born September 8, 1923, to Edgar Atherton Mayhew and Bertha (Pruitt) Mayhew. Married Rudolph Alexander Wharton on June 4, 1950. A registered Republican voter. Mother Bertha P. Mayhew died March 7, 1940; father Edgar Atherton Mayhew died February 2, 1949. Present address, 17 Howe Street.

I turned to the next card. MAYHEW, Eulalie Veronica. Born August 19, 1924, to Edgar Atherton Mayhew and Bertha (Pruitt) Mayhew. Lived at 1172 Abbott Road until November 1953. Present address, 3394 Ling Lane, Riverside, California.

I heard footsteps. I flipped more cards, quickly, to M-A-Z. MAZALETTI, Alphonso, born . . .

"How are you doing?" Mrs. Davis peered over my shoulder.

I looked up sadly. "Zero. I couldn't find anything close. I guess Mom will just have to get more information for me. There's a cousin in Copenhagen, if she'll write to her . . ."

"Yes, it really does help to have the spelling. I hope you'll excuse me, but I have to look up something, there's someone on the telephone."

"Sure." I gave way, watched her as she deftly went through the B-O section, found what she wanted. "I just wanted to say, thanks anyway."

Card in hand, she beamed at me. "You're very welcome."

Almost out of the Town Clerk's office, I had another thought, waited until she was off the phone. "One other thing, Mrs. Davis . . ."

"Yes?"

"We bought our house from the Pinkhams. You don't know where they moved to, do you?"

"Pinkham? Which Pinkham?"

I looked as sheepish as I felt. "I don't remember his first name but they lived at 20 Howe Street until this year."

She gave me a motherly look. "I'll see." And she came back with Horatio Pinkham, 829 Beau Boulevard, Brewster.

"Thanks again, Mrs. Davis. You're a doll."

She grinned. "Remember that when I run for re-election next March."

I stopped by the police station and found Elihu at the

desk. "What happened to you?" he asked, looking at my bandaged hand. I told him.

"Just wait till the full moon," he said wisely. "That's when they really come out from their booby hatches."

"Is the chief busy?"

He glanced at his switchboard. "He's on the telephone. I heard you were in on that Farley kid pick-up."

"Right. How's the follow-up going?"

"They released him to the custody of his parents. This Rooney is coming in to sign the complaint sometime today. In my opinion, the guy was asking for it. The kid said he'd left his keys in the ignition."

"They don't take advice, do they? It isn't easy enough to snatch a car what with slam pullers and slim jims, they've got to go around leaving their keys, doors unlocked."

Elihu looked down. "The chief's off the phone now."

"Ask him if I can see him for a few minutes."

The answer was yes. The chief was leaning back in his swivel chair, rubbing his eyes with his knuckles. "I'm getting old," he told me. "One of these days . . ." He straightened up. "You did a good job on that car theft. We'll let you know when we need you in court."

"Okay." I sat down across from him. I didn't know exactly how to put it to him, so I said slowly, "Remember when you talked to Mrs. Wharton?"

"Mrs. Wharton?" A small frown appeared between his eyes. "Something new on that?"

"No. I mean, no more letters. Not that I know of. I do have something new on the telephone caller, though. I'll get to that in a minute. When you talked to Mrs.

Wharton, what did you ask her exactly? Things like when she left Wellesley, how she got to California?"

"Well, no. I just asked if she was okay . . ." The frown reappeared, deepened. "What are you getting at?"

"Nothing probably." I held up my bandaged paw. "I've got a purple heart coming and it's left me on the defensive." I grinned, let it slide away. "My wife says I'm a bulldog. With a police mentality."

Torrence bristled. "I hope you don't get any ideas that I didn't check thoroughly, that I would whitewash Wharton just because he's a selectman . . ."

"No." I spoke quickly. "I didn't get any ideas like that."

Mollified, he said, "Well, I hope not. That's not my way. There's some people in this town who try to get to me, but—I don't play that game."

"I can tell that by looking and listening."

"Okay. I just wanted to set things straight. In case. I take it you've got an itch."

"An itch?"

"That's what I call it. An itch I can't scratch. Keeps me up nights, sometimes. A feeling that something's out of kilter, off the mark."

"Yes, that's a good description. An itch. Was Rudolph Wharton born here?"

"No." He sat forward now, elbows on his desk. Quite a neat desk, I noticed, unlike Captain Granger's. "He came here after the war. World War II, I mean. That was *the* war to me."

"Came here from where?"

"New York State, I believe. He showed up at Babson College, Institute it was then, on the GI Bill. Joined the

Veterans of Foreign Wars here, he'd been a first lieutenant in the Army Air Corps, and that was the way I first met him. Started going out with the Mayhew girls, married one of them and settled down. Twenty-five years later, he's a selectman and owns half the town. One of those classic success stories, don't you think?"

"You say he dated the Mayhew girls? Both of them?"

"Well, kind of. I'm older, you know, so I wouldn't be sure of the details but my wife and I used to run into the three of them at Ken's all the time. Both of them looking at him as though he were God."

I had my notebook out, was idly drawing lopsided hearts as I listened. "Ken's?"

"You haven't been to Ken's? It's a fancy steakhouse on the Worcester Turnpike, a few miles up in Framingham. You ought to take your wife there sometime. In those days it was the hangout for the twenty-and-up set. Good steak dinner for $2.95. With a great salad. Half of Wellesley went there." He squinted at me. "What have you got on your mind?"

I drew an arrow through one of my hearts. "I don't know. My curiosity bump—I guess you could say it's itching. What did the Mayhews look like? I'd like to get hold of a picture of them."

"Well, they were—and still are, I guess—good-looking blondes. To tell the truth, I was kind of surprised that Rudy chose Ernestine. She was the quiet one, Eulalie was the bubbler. Miss Personality herself, that was Eulalie. Seemed like she went out of her way to make everybody like her. But maybe in the long run, Ernestine was the comfortable one. You know what I mean." He shifted his weight. "A picture, huh? You might talk Constance Giordi out of one but on second thought that would be harder than talking a dog off a meat wagon. Constance is a tartar. The only other thing I can think of would be the Library. Seems to me they have all the Wellesley Senior High School yearbooks there. The Mayhews would have graduated around 1940. Maybe Ernestine in 1940 and Eulalie in 1941. Something like that."

"Constance Giordi, you said. Who would she be?"

"She was the Mayhews' housekeeper. Watchdog would be more like it. And I'm not too sure but what her bite is even worse than her bark. I gave her a parking ticket one time, before I was chief, and boy, you never heard such a tongue-lashing as she gave me."

"Where does she live?"

"With her old mother over in Back Bay. Oak Street. Built herself a nice little house when Ernestine got married and Eulalie went off to California."

"But you don't recommend that I go see her?"

"That's up to you. I had a little talk with her when this letter business came up. A little talk is just what I mean. I said something like, Miss Giordi, have you heard from Ernestine? Her husband says she's left him and gone to California. And she said, in effect, where Ernestine went was her own business and I should mind mine. I don't know about you, but I'm a devout coward when it comes to little old ladies with tart tongues and Miss Constance Giordi brings out the believer in me." He gave me a wry smile.

I snapped my notebook shut and put it away. "The other thing I had on my mind, the telephone nut. He called my house yesterday." I told Torrence the details. "So the question is, how did he get my number?"

"From information?"

"It's unpublished."

Torrence's eyes gleamed. "Is that a fact? Very interesting."

"Yes. Very. I'm going to keep my eyes and ears open. It looks as though we might be acquainted with the caller in some way. A neighbor? A repairman? One of the guys that hung the new wallpaper?"

Torrence scratched the side of his nose thoughtfully. "He's been varying his pattern, hasn't he? That Selene business was a funny one."

"Wasn't it? Well, thanks, Chief. I'll be in touch."

"If you need any help, holler." He stood up and offered his hand.

I shook it, had an afterthought. "What do you know about a group called the Drama-tics?"

Torrence looked blank for a moment. "Some acting club, isn't it? There's a couple of them in town, the Wellesley Players and this other outfit. The wife and I are television addicts, we seldom get out even to a movie and with some of the stuff they're showing on the screen these days, can that be bad?"

I grinned. "I guess the only thing you're missing out on is the popcorn."

The Wellesley Free Library was just down the street from the police station, a smart-looking brick building of modern design. I strolled in and asked about the high school annuals, was directed to the proper section. It didn't take me long to find the right ones, Torrence had been off by only a year, Ernestine was graduated in 1941 and Eulalie in 1942. Under Ernestine's photo were the words, "Still waters run deep" and beneath Eulalie's it said, "Miss Vivacity, best dressed girl, cheer leader, everybody's pal." If you didn't look too closely, they might have been the same girl. Identical blond hairdos with pompadours on the top and long page-boy arrangements hanging down. Ernestine had a more pensive look while Eulalie's eyes had a definite sparkle.

As Torrence had said about another matter, very interesting. I looked over the rest of each page, such generally solemn faces. Lester Martin. Clarence Masters. Nella Mawhinney. Where were they now, some thirty years later?

I put the books back and drove home. California was a long way away, for all practical purposes it might as well have been the moon. And telephone conversations—what did that prove? Unless . . . An idea came to me and I played with it, found myself in my own driveway before I knew it.

It wasn't a world beater of an idea but it might prove something. No harm, as far as I could see, in trying.

"Oh, Knute, I'm glad you're home," Brenda greeted me. "You can stay with the baby while I run down to the grocery store. I've just discovered I'm out of coffee."

"Okay. Where is the heir apparent?"

"Sleeping, as usual. I shouldn't complain, but he certainly does like his sack time."

"That's the way he makes up for those two o'clock feedings. Would that we could. Go ahead, I'll hold the fort."

"I won't be long."

"Take your time." When the car had left the driveway, I went to the telephone. Now, I figured, was as good a time as any. I dialed long distance information, was routed to the Riverside, California, area. "I'd like the phone number of Eulalie Mayhew," I told the operator. The phone would be in her name, no reason to change it just because her sister had moved in with her.

"E. Mayhew," answered the operator. "We have an E. Mayhew on Ling Lane. Would that be it?"

"Yes, that would be it."

"Would you care to take it down?"

"I would." And I did, hung up, and dialed the number myself. After three rings, someone picked up the phone on the other end and said, "Hello?"

"Miss Mayhew?" I asked. "Eulalie?"

There was a slight pause. "Yes. Who is this?"

"This is Lester Martin from Wellesley. Remember me?"

"Lester Martin? From Wellesley?" A most doubtful tone.

"Yes, I was in the class of 1941, a year ahead of you in school."

"School? Wellesley High School?"

"That's right. Is Ernestine there? I've got a very important message for Ernestine."

Another pause, slightly longer. "Yes. Just a moment." I heard the phone being put down, a faint sound of footsteps. Everybody's pal had lost some of her friendly manner it seemed. There were footsteps returning then and someone said, "Hello." The hello sounded much like the previous one, natural, I supposed in sisters, not quite the same, but certainly similar.

"This is Lester Martin, Ernestine."

"Oh, yes. Lester Martin. From Wellesley High." If I ever heard pretense, here it was.

"You don't remember me. Well, it's been some time, I've been living in Sudbury, you see, and when you haven't heard of a fella for almost thirty years. I was the funny-looking guy with glasses. Now do you remember?"

"Oh, yes. Lester Martin. How are you, Lester?" She still didn't know Lester Martin from Adam. Again natural enough. You don't remember everybody you went to school with.

"Just fine, Ernestine. Listen, the reason I'm calling is because we're planning a reunion this fall and we want to make it a hundred percent, so we've got this committee and everybody was given a list of names to personally contact and you're on my list but imagine my surprise when I found out you don't live in Wellesley any more, you're in California. Well, I said to my wife, I don't care if it costs money or not, I'm going to call Ernestine."

"That's very nice of you, Lester. When is the reunion?"

"Thanksgiving Day. The old football rivalry, you know." Who the devil did Wellesley play on Thanksgiving? I couldn't recall. "We'll make it a real homecoming."

"Thanksgiving Day. Well. I don't know. I was considering a trip to Europe this fall. Who else is going?"

"Oh, Clarence Masters and Nella Mawhinney, I've got the M's . . ."

"Is Patsy Oliver going?"

Who was Patsy Oliver, some school chum of hers, I imagined. "Yes, I think so. She's not on my list, but I think somebody said so . . ."

"I'll have to think about it, Lester, and let you know. Where can I get in touch with you?"

"I'll send you a letter with all the details. You can look it over and make up your mind. It's sure been good to talk to you, Ernestine. A lot of water's gone over the dam, huh?"

Dryly, "Yes. A lot of water. Thank you for calling, Lester."

"You betcha. Still waters run deep, right, Ernestine?"

"I beg your pardon?"

"You know—water over the dam and still waters run deep? Just a little play on words. My wife says I'm hopeless."

"Yes. I see what you mean." Her laugh was less than hearty.

"Well, so long, Ernestine."

"Goodbye, Lester."

And I stood there after I'd hung up, thinking what an unsatisfactory instrument the telephone could be. Now, if we'd only had that TV-phone Tel and Tel was always talking about.

Except that—she'd have been able to see me, too.

"One more time," I said aloud and then dialed a second California number. I had an old friend in L.A., Detective Jess Dyer, who would do me a favor. Just a quick look around the house on Ling Lane and a little checking with the neighbors. He said right on and I said how are you and then I had to tell him about Brenda and the baby and when I finally hung up I thought that Brenda would have a fit when she saw this month's phone bill.

We had just finished dinner and Brenda was telling me about a conversation she'd had with Gloria that afternoon. "She sounded so funny, Knute, I just don't know what to make of it, as though she didn't much want to talk to me . . ."

The doorbell rang. I sighed and said, "I'll get it."

Mercy Bird stood on the porch and the moment she saw me, she told me, "Algernon's gone. Somebody kidnapped him."

"Kidnapped Algernon? Are you sure . . . ?" I came out on the porch with her. She grabbed at my arm, pulling me toward the steps.

"I don't know, I think things like that. Maybe he broke his rope, come and see—he's gone and he's like a baby, an innocent, he's never been out in traffic, we've got to find him . . ."

The rope had been severed, I couldn't be sure in the semidarkness, but it looked as though it had been broken. "You'd better call the police station," I advised. "The cruisers can be on the lookout for him. And while you're doing that, I'll take my car and drive around the neighborhood. How long has he been gone?"

She looked ready to cry. "I don't know, I was working, concentrating, I just don't know."

"All right, we'll find him, Mercy. You call 235-1212 and I'll get going." I hurried back to my place, stuck my head in through the back door and told Brenda.

"Algernon? Oh dear. Mercy will be so upset if anything happens to him."

"I'll be back as soon as I can." And as I backed the car out, I saw Brenda going across to Mercy's house, perhaps she could calm her down. I'd never guessed that Mercy had a nerve in that ample body.

I went up Howe to Curve Street, around Curve, back onto Weston Road, that's where the nearest concentration of traffic was, but no sign.

I came back to Howe Street, up over the hill onto Crest Road, no lumbering canine form that I could see and it would be hard to miss Algernon even in the failing light. I debated which way to go. He could be anywhere.

I turned onto Summit, found myself in a maze of small cross streets, some of which I'd never taken before. It was getting darker, much darker and very quickly and I was nearing the Turnpike. If the big dog had gotten that far, over to Route 9 where the speed limit varied from 40 to 60 and cars went even faster than that . . . I didn't want to think about it.

I nosed out onto 9, half expecting to see a bulky body lying on the pavement but, thank God, didn't; came back toward the village, found myself on Oak Street, wasn't that where Constance Giordi lived? Yes, it was. I came out at Linden Street, looked right and left and turned left to the Linden Shopping Center. Lots of cars in the shopping center parking lot, Friendly's Ice Cream was the attraction and there on the wide sidewalk in front of Friendly's was a clump of people, youngsters from the shape of them, crowded around something.

I pulled up and got out. Algernon smiled up at me from among his new friends, tongue lolling. A short length of rope hung from his collar.

I patted his head. "Well, old fella, you had us worried," I told him.

"Is he your dog, mister?" asked one of the group.

"Not mine exactly. My neighbor's. She's upset. Algernon," I said to the dog.

"Algernon," the kids smiled, laughed, or giggled, they appreciated that. One of them said, "He's a nice dog."

"Yes, he is. Come on, nice dog." I took hold of the short length of rope, but Algernon didn't want to go. He was enjoying himself, obviously.

The kids began to push at his rear quarters while I tugged at him from the front and, between us, we got him into my car. He hung his massive head out the window, slobbering over the side, and beamed at them.

"Goodbye, Algernon," they chorused and as I backed out I heard one of them echo, "Algernon!" and they cracked up.

I drove right into Mercy's drive and took Algernon up to the door. This side of the house had an enclosed porch and its outer door was locked. I banged on it, trying to see in. The lights were dim inside, I couldn't make out much other than a couple of shapes that looked like cardboard cartons and another that seemed to be a bench.

"Who is it?" called Mercy from inside.

"It's Knute. I've found Algernon."

"Wait a minute." She sounded different, quite different from the way she had when I'd left her, detached. She came out, unlatched the porch door and reached out for Algernon. "Thank you," she spoke almost abruptly.

"You're welcome," I said uncertainly. "He was down at Friendly's. I guess he got hungry for an ice cream cone."

"Thank you," she said again, gave Algernon a yank and took him in, leaving me standing there with what felt like egg on my face.

I put the car away and went into my house from the back. "What's with Mercy?" I asked Brenda without knowing just where she was. "I found the dog and she acted as though . . ." I stopped in the living-room archway. Brenda sat in the Boston rocker with a most peculiar look on her face.

"Oh, Knute."

"What's happened?"

"I wish I'd never gone over there, but I thought she'd be so upset and maybe I could help . . ."

"And?"

"I walked up on the porch and opened the door, called Mercy, she didn't hear me, I think she was on the phone, but the living-room door was ajar so I walked in but the room was empty, there isn't much furniture in it either except for this huge roll-top desk and I couldn't help noticing it, it was right there in front of me . . ." She looked miserable at the thought.

"What was right there in front of you?" I demanded impatiently.

"You said the letters were made of pasted words from newspapers and I just couldn't help seeing—she'd pasted a line or so on, it said, 'Somebody's covering up, it was murder.'"

I let myself sink slowly down into the wing chair. "A letter about Wharton? You mean that Mercy is the poison-pen letter writer? Mercy?"

She nodded her head hopelessly. "She has to be."

"Did she say anything? Did she know you saw it?"

She looked even more miserable. "I'm afraid so. She didn't say a word, but she came and stood in front of the desk, switched some papers around, muttered something about forgetting to lock the door, and then she asked me right out, 'What are you doing here? Don't you know I don't like people in my house?'"

"Mercy Bird," I said softly. "My God." I felt as bad as Brenda did.

"What are you going to do?"

I thought about it. "Talk to her first, I guess."

"And then what? You're not going to have her arrested, are you, Knute? I know it's a terrible thing to do, write letters like that, but she must be ill, she needs help."

"I'll talk to her," I said again and pulled myself up from the chair. My hand, misused, gave a twinge.

Algernon now occupied the glassed porch. He struggled up when I knocked, woofed and then, recognizing me, wagged his heavy tail.

"Who is it?" Mercy asked me for the second time.

"It's Knute. I want to talk to you."

"I've gone to bed."

"Then get up and let me in. Unless you want me to yell at you from out here."

Algernon made friendly whining sounds and tried to get through the glass.

I heard her moving around inside and, at last, the inner door opened. It must be hot as hades in there, I thought, with all those doors locked. We stood looking at each other across the porch. She could see my face by the bare bulb that lit her porch door and steps. I couldn't see hers, it was in shadow.

She came then, slowly, across the six-foot space, pushed Algernon aside and unlocked the porch door. I came in, squeezed past the enthusiastic Saint Bernard, and followed her inside. Brenda's description had been apt, there wasn't much furniture inside. A very ancient Oriental on the floor was too small for the room. There were a couple of overstuffed chairs that reminded me of the ones my mother had when I was a kid, mohair, I think. And the roll-top desk which predominated.

"My mother was sick a long time," said Mercy almost angrily. "I had to get by without a lot of things to pay for her care."

I chose one of the mohair chairs and sat in it. She had put on a bathrobe, terrycloth, a sort of faded pink color that once maybe had been blue. She didn't look at me but sat in the other chair. Algernon, who had come in with us, sat adoringly at her feet and panted. He was right. It was hot in here.

"Why?" I asked peremptorily. "Why did you write those letters accusing Wharton?"

There was a long silence and I thought she didn't intend to answer. But then, in a faraway voice: "I know he killed her. I know. I didn't see it, but I know. And somebody had to pay attention. I knew they wouldn't believe me if I told them. They think I'm—strange."

"By they, I take it you mean the police."

She nodded that head of wildly curling hair.

I stared at her forcefully. "What makes you believe Mrs. Wharton is dead?"

She closed her lips in a firm line. "I can't give you what you call evidence. I know. That's all."

"Your ESP again?" I tried to keep the sarcasm out of my voice, that would get me nowhere.

"Call it that if you like. Ernestine and I were friends of a sort. She was a kind, gentle lady on the surface but strong, very strong underneath. If she'd meant to leave him, she would have indicated it. I would have known. But she didn't. I never could understand, but she loved him. It was very mysterious." Another nod. "That's the word, mysterious."

"And you took it upon yourself to accuse the man of murder just because his wife didn't tell you her troubles?"

Stubborn lines formed around her mouth. "I would have known." She blinked at me. "How do you know I'm not right? Has anybody really looked? Dug up his cellar? Looked into his trunks or gone into his flower beds? If a man like Wharton wanted to get rid of a body, he'd find a way. But nobody's done anything about it. Nobody cares."

"Nobody's done anything about it because the woman is alive and well in California. Chief Torrence had a letter from her, has talked to her on the telephone. I've called her myself."

Her eyes narrowed. "You called her? Then you are suspicious! There are ways to get around anything, you know. Just read a few mystery books, you'll see what I mean. Ernestine has a sister who looks like her, sounds like her for all I know. He could have sweet-talked the sister into covering up . . ."

"Now, Mercy, be reasonable. By what means could a man get his wife's sister to pretend her sister was living if she were dead? And as for this look-alike, sound-alike business, that only works in books."

She shook her head emphatically. "He could do it. For one thing, I've heard that the sister was crazy about him. I'll bet you didn't know that."

I all but groaned. She had a fixation and that was the truth. What was I going to do with her? Wharton could press charges, but did I want that to happen? She needed a doctor, the State would put her in psychotherapy, all right, but in an institution? Maybe if I talked to Wharton, got him to agree . . .

Brenda was waiting anxiously for me. "What happened? What did she say? What are you going to do?"

I told her.

"Oh, Knute!" She threw her arms around me. "You're the dearest man in the world."

I held her close. "Well, the dearest man in the world is the tiredest man in the world right now. I'm going to bed. Maybe in the morning I can think better."

She drew her head back, kissed me on the cheek, then

wondered, "I suppose it's because she's a writer, has that
kind of imagination, but why do you suppose she's so
set on this awful thing?"

I turned her around and we started up the stairs arm
in arm. "She's alone, for one thing. No one else to think
about except herself, her dog, and her neighbors."

Brenda stopped abruptly on the first landing, caused
me to stop, too. "You know, I would almost believe her
if it weren't so impossible. And if it weren't Rudolph
Wharton. Because, you see, I don't believe that Mercy
lies."

"Woman!" I ejaculated. "A bag of bones and a hank of
hair and a skinful of intuition. Mercy 'knows' that Wharton killed his wife, you 'know' that Wharton wouldn't
and you 'know' that Mercy doesn't lie. Well, she isn't
lying as she sees it. She believes it and I'll tell you one
thing, after I talk to Wharton tomorrow, I wash my
hands of this whole mess. Who said it was peaceful in
the country? Bah, humbug."

"Maybe that's just as well," there was an edge to her
voice and I thought, oh boy, here we go again.

I moved on ahead of her, I was too beat to joust at
windmills. "I wonder . . ." said Brenda behind me.

"You wonder what?"

"I'm not really talking to you, I'm talking to myself."
God, she could be feisty.

I said patiently, "You wonder what?"

"I wonder if Rudolph Wharton could have killed his
wife?"

I bit back my answer, asked instead, "But I thought
you liked the man?"

"Well, I do," said Brenda reasonably. "He's been very nice to me. But that doesn't prove anything, actually, doesn't mean he couldn't have done it. Tempers flare, you know, and accidents do happen. You should know by this time, Knute"—she left the bedroom door behind us open so that she could hear Leif in the night—"that just because you happen to like somebody doesn't mean he can do no wrong."

I stared at her in wonder, went into the bathroom and closed that door firmly. A hot bath, that was the ticket. A hot bath and a couple of aspirins. Some days it just didn't pay to get up.

I found Wharton in his office which was in a building that housed a bank, a drugstore, and a department store. It seemed he owned that block, too.

He had a secretary in the outer office, a slim little thing with doe eyes who looked as though she were straight out of business school. "Whom shall I say is calling?" was her reply to my request to see Mr. Wharton.

I told her. She picked up the telephone, pushed a button and gave my name. "You can go right in," she said when she'd finished. "Through that door."

I thanked her and went in. Wharton's office was wood-paneled and wall-to-wall carpeted. He stood when I entered, asked me to sit down, wanted to know what he could do for me. All very cordial.

I told him. This was my day for telling people.

He resumed his chair, swiveled it and looked out of his picture window. Beyond was a church and a cemetery. The sky was blue, accented with a pair of fluffy clouds, the trees were leafy and green, the grass luxuriant. Wonderful Wellesley. Adding a colorful touch was a discarded Budweiser can nestling next to a tombstone, red and white against the green. A reminder of the times. A piece of ugly amid the beautiful.

"Poor Mercy." There was infinite pity in Wharton's voice. "She never quite got over her mother's death. They were very close." He turned his chair back to me. "She blames me for it, perhaps she's told you. I have always thought that strange. It's natural enough to blame someone, the doctor, the fates. But just because I own the nursing home . . ." He made a helpless gesture.

I wished I could read the mask he wore for a face better. "What do you want to do about her?" I asked. "Press charges?"

"Press charges?" He pushed his lower lip over his top one. "What would happen to her?"

I shrugged, elaborately casual. "It's my opinion she needs psychotherapy."

"Isn't there some way she could get that without pressing charges?"

"Would she seek it herself? And can she afford it? I don't know. She writes books, but from the looks of things she's not rolling in money."

"Would you ask her? You could tell her that if she'd have voluntary treatment, I'd be willing to"—another gesture with his hands, they were graceful hands, especially for a man—"forgive and forget."

"I can try." I didn't want the job, I wanted out, but who else was there?

"I'd appreciate it." He smiled that illuminating smile. Maybe Brenda had been right in her assessment, I guessed he was a damned good-looking man. "Oh, by the way," he sobered. "I had a telephone call from my sister-in-law this morning. She's coming on to Wellesley."

"Is she?" Now, why would Eulalie do that, I wondered.

He read my mind. "My wife has had a sudden urge to take a trip to Hawaii. Flew out this morning. Eulalie called right after, said she wanted to talk to me. She's worried about Ernestine, she says."

"Is she?" I sounded like a broken record.

"Yes. For several reasons. One being that she had a peculiar phone call from Wellesley. Eulalie thinks it might have been on the level, but Ernestine said it was a crank. Something about a school reunion and she was suspicious right off, I don't know why, but she asked if Patsy Oliver were coming and the caller said he thought she was."

I frowned. "So?"

"Well, you see, Patsy Oliver was a very well-known name when the girls were in school. Only Patsy Oliver was Patrick C. Oliver, you see, so that when the caller said 'she' was coming, Ernestine became very wary. Eulalie says she's been very morose since she came to California. Eulalie wanted me to come out there, but I told her I couldn't. She said couldn't or wouldn't? I had to answer honestly that I wasn't sure."

"Is it"—treading on thin ice—"something that can't be patched up between the two of you?"

"Patched up." He spoke the words as though he were examining them. "Such an ugly phrase. If Ernestine were to return of her own volition . . . I told Eulalie that but she said she didn't think she would. And I responded that it is most difficult for a man to forgive rejection. That's what she did, you know. Simply packed up and left without explanation. If we had quarreled, if there had been a reason, something I'd done, but this way— it was as if she'd simply had enough of me, wanted no more."

Another delicate question, only how does one ask delicately about money? "No financial problems?" Let him take it whichever way he wished.

He raised aristocratic eyebrows. "Ernestine is a very wealthy woman, perhaps you didn't know. Or, do you mean me? I am quite comfortable, thank you. All of the property is in our joint names. Whatever she decides, I will receive my share."

"She hasn't asked for a divorce?"

"She hasn't asked for anything. The only communication I've had is that letter in reply to my cry for help."

"Don't you think that's odd?"

"Normally, perhaps, but then you don't know Ernestine. She is very quiet, keeps things to herself. A private, most private individual."

I studied him. A man above average, obviously, in appearance, intelligence. If I'd been asked to describe him in a flattering word, the word would have been dignified, meanly translated as cold. And another word, also not flattering, would have been evasive. He specialized in dignity but it came out icy evasion. Well, why should he tell me his problems? I had no authority, he had committed no crime. To him, I supposed, I came across as a nosy neighbor, nothing else. And when I came right down to it, that's what I was. The cop mentality thing—only, damn it, the man lived right across the street from my wife and child and he gave me goose bumps!

"Thanks for your time," I said, rising. "I'll carry through with Mercy."

"I'm grateful for that." He stood and offered his hand. The shake was perfunctory, his fault or mine? He came to the door with me, led me past the little secretary, said, "I'm going to be gone for a few minutes, Miss Kelly," and walked me out to the street. I should give my regards to Brenda, he told me, and I said I would. He turned toward the post office and I turned and went into the bank.

I asked for the president, was directed to him. I told him who I was and produced my Boston ID. I was assisting the Wellesley police with an investigation, I said, and I wanted some information. How could he be sure of that? he asked cautiously and I suggested that he telephone the chief. I sat around while the call was put through, my status verified.

"I would like to know if Ernestine Wharton has an account here, if it's a separate or joint checking account and whether she has drawn any money on it since January."

Mr. Dawson looked at me over the tops of his half glasses. He thought for a long moment, came to a conclusion and picked up his phone to call some inner recess of the bank that housed bookkeeping. We stared at each other and made small talk while we waited for an answer. I could tell that he was filled with curiosity, but his position kept him from asking what he considered impertinent questions.

After a few minutes, the phone rang and he jotted down some notes. Hanging up, he said, "Mrs. Wharton does have a separate account. She has written no checks since January 5 when she withdrew five hundred dollars."

Five hundred dollars. In six months. How far could one go on five hundred dollars? But there were such things as credit cards, I supposed she could have flown by credit card . . . "Thank you very much, Mr. Dawson," I said and went out to my car. My injured hand was on the mend, I noted. I could use it on the steering wheel to some extent.

I turned off Washington onto Kingsbury and then onto Linden. Another visit was on my list this free day. A stop on Oak Street.

The sheer curtain against the door window jerked.

"We don't want any," said a querulous female voice.

"Miss Giordi," I said, and then, "I'm not selling anything. I just want to speak to you a moment."

"Who are you?" I could barely make out the shape of a head against the glass curtain.

"My name is Severson. Knute Severson."

"I don't know any Seversons."

"No, you don't know me . . ." A little girl, walking down the street, stopped and looked curiously at me. I lowered my voice. "You don't know me, but I live across the street from Mr. Wharton."

"I don't wish to speak about Rudolph Wharton."

"But it's not Mr. Wharton I want to talk about, Miss Giordi," the little girl produced a lollipop, removed the paper and began to lick it, never taking her eyes off me. "It's about Mrs. Wharton. Ernestine Mayhew."

There was no response and I thought briefly that she'd gone away. I had my hand up, ready to knock again when there was a loud click, the sound of a key very definitely unlocking, and the door opened inward.

"Come in, come in," said the whiny voice. "Don't stand there yelling through the door where all the neighbors can know my business."

I stepped inside. The Oriental runner under my feet was immaculate, looked expensive. Thick, well-padded. The eggshell walls of the hall looked newly papered, never touched by human hands. The *pièce de résistance* was a gold cross, good-sized, hanging halfway between the front door and the archway.

Constance Giordi was short, but she made up for that in girth. She was round, body, arms, face, as though someone had rolled cylinders of clay into balls and stuck them all together. Her eyes were black, what my mother used to call snapping black, her hair was black, too, drawn up into a coronet braid that made a final circular line atop her head. While I looked at her, she looked at me. Two strange cats, and then from the direction of the archway, someone spoke, asking a question that I didn't understand, speaking Italian.

Miss Giordi answered in that language and the other voice, also female but sounding ancient, said something else. "Come," Miss Giordi spoke brusquely to me, "my mother is getting senile. She is ninety-three. She thinks she must meet everyone who comes to the door."

I followed Miss Giordi through the archway, found an antique-filled room, all polished woods and elegant chairs with lace doilies and, enthroned on one of them with a high back, the original of Miss Giordi, equally round, equally black-eyed and her dark hair was streaked with white. Her apple face looked shriveled. Too much time in sun and shade.

"What did you say your name was?" Miss Giordi asked.

I told her and she repeated my name for her mother, added an Italian sentence. The old lady looked pleased and indicated that I should sit. "I told her you were a friend of the Mayhews," Miss Giordi explained grudgingly. "I doubt that that's so, but I had to tell her something."

I sat as directed. Mrs. Giordi beamed and nodded and Miss Giordi remained standing. Across the room, above her head, was a brightly colored picture of a bleeding heart. Above the fireplace was a mirror with wide gold Florentine frame and on the mantel below it were groups of pictures, many tinted, some in black and white plus a few colored photographs. "I don't actually know Ernestine and Eulalie," I confessed, "but I'm concerned about them. Have you heard from Ernestine since she went to California?"

The black eyes, like a falcon's, were hooded like a falcon's. "What business is it of yours?"

"I just want to know if you're satisfied that she's all right."

The little old lady was looking from me to Constance as though she were watching a tennis match.

"Why wouldn't she be all right?" asked Miss Giordi belligerently.

I'd come armed with a copy of one of the letters Mercy had sent the police. I took it out of my pocket and offered it to her. Her mother wanted to see it, too, so she held it down for her to look at, read it as she did so. Looking up, she asked suspiciously, "What does this mean?"

"It means that someone thinks Rudolph Wharton did

away with his wife. That she didn't go to California at all. Have you heard from her?"

The black eyes blazed. "Nonsense! She told me she was leaving. She telephoned me just before she left, in January. 'I've had enough,' she said, 'I'm leaving him, Constance. And I'll see how well he does on unemployment.' And I said, 'Good riddance. Don't leave him a thing. You should have done it years ago.'"

Her mother interrupted with a question and Constance translated for her. The old lady nodded her head wisely.

"You say she'd had enough. Enough of what? They'd been married some twenty years—why, suddenly . . . ?"

"You're the police?" The question was abrupt.

"Yes, but not here. Boston police. Only that doesn't have much to do with it. I have no actual jurisdiction. But he lives across the street from us, my wife's had him to dinner."

The brilliant jet eyes narrowed. "You watch your wife."

I blinked. "Watch my wife?"

"He is a woman chaser. Was, and is, and always will be. I told her when she married him. I said, let Eulalie have him if you must have him around, Eulalie can handle him better. But she went against me, the only time she went against me. And regretted it. Oh, yes, she regretted it." She turned, made an arc, sat in a chair with grape carving alongside the fireplace. "She made her bed," she muttered to herself, and then to me, "You look as though you doubt me."

"I'm—surprised. He seems—he acts so respectable."

Her heavy dark eyebrows moved up. "Of course. You don't think a Mayhew would marry an obvious bum, do you? He is very clever, but I can see through him. His little politenesses. Especially to the ladies. Thought he could get around me, too. But he couldn't." She looked down at her lap. "So they pensioned me off. He didn't want me around. In the prime of my life. I pleaded with Ernestine, but she was blinded. They could have lived in the Mayhew house, I could have cared for her, for them. But no, he talked her into what she called a simple life. A small house, one she could take care of. No servants, he didn't want servants because if he had servants she would have chosen me above all, and he knew that I knew him."

I glanced at the mantel, at one of the large pictures, a tinted picture where the mouth was like cherry wine and the eyes like iris and the hair spun gold. "Is that Ernestine?"

"It is."

"Where's Eulalie?"

"Ernestine was my favorite just as she was her papa's favorite. She was everybody's favorite."

Mother Giordi put in her two liras' worth, it seemed that while she spoke Italian, she understood some English because she mentioned the name Wharton and when she was through, Constance nodded.

She said, "He convinced Ernestine that I wanted to stifle her, to keep her as a child. He turned her against me for a while, she would not believe a word I said against him. Not until later, much later." She stood up on fat little legs and went to the street window, looked out through heavy lacy curtains. "And so I lost her. She was like my own daughter and I lost her."

"Have you heard from her since she left?" She never had answered my original question.

"No." She didn't turn so I couldn't see her face but there was emotion in her voice. "Not a word. Not a word since the telephone call in January."

"You said you told her to let Eulalie have him. Was Eulalie in love with him, too?"

She did face me now. "With Eulalie you never knew. So much put on. They were, in some ways, two of a kind."

"But when he married Ernestine, it was so long ago, was Eulalie angry? She moved out to the coast shortly after that, didn't she?"

Constance Giordi shrugged. "They had no estrangement, if that's what you mean. Eulalie was used to Ernestine having her way, it had always been so. I am certain they discussed the matter, Ernestine was like that, everything out in the open, a very honest child. And once I came into the room where they were together and Eulalie's face was crimson, as I recall she held something, a poker, something in her hand, and Ernestine's eyes were filled with tears. But whatever happened, whatever was said, Ernestine married him and Eulalie stood up for her." She spoke quickly to her mother, then asked accusingly, "Why have not you investigated this letter?"

"We have. Chief Torrence telephoned, got a letter from Ernestine. He checked the airlines, someone named Ernestine Wharton flew from Boston on January tenth to Los Angeles. And I've talked to them myself, even called a friend in Los Angeles to look into it. We've done all we can."

She moved behind her mother's chair, tapped on its

high wooden sides with pudgy fingers. "But still you have doubts?"

I nodded.

"You say she wrote a letter. Do you have the letter?"

"No, but I'm sure I can get it."

"Why didn't that idiot Torrence bring it to me? Why didn't he do that?"

"Because he was satisfied. At the time, he was satisfied."

"But not now?"

I thought about that. "I believe he is still satisfied. But those letters"—I indicated the one she'd left on the table —"make him uneasy. Wharton is one of his bosses, an important man in the town, Torrence is on edge about that. Because the letter writer is so positive and so persistent, you see, and he feels that Wharton expected him to apprehend the letter writer right off. I guess that's why he told me about it, it bothers him that: a, Mrs. Wharton seems to be all right; b, the writer kept insisting she is dead; and c, he couldn't stop the writer from annoying Wharton."

"But you—you go further than Torrence. Why? Why do you come to me to talk to me about my Ernestine? It is an imposition, you know. I could have told you nothing." Her gypsy eyes were penetrating.

I had to tell her honestly, "I don't know. I've asked myself. I've accused myself of being prejudiced against Wharton. He's so damn'—I beg your pardon—suave."

Her mother looked up at Constance curiously and Constance spoke rapidly. Again the little old lady nodded.

"Can you get Ernestine's letter for me?" asked Miss Giordi.

"I think so."

"Let me see it. I can tell you if she wrote it. You could not fool me about Ernestine's handwriting."

I felt an absurd sense of relief. If she said the letter was from Ernestine, I could let go of this awkward bone I'd been carrying around in my bulldog teeth. Chief Torrence should have come to Miss Giordi in the first place, that's what I would have done. Curious, I asked as I was leaving, "Is there any reason that the chief should be in awe of you, Miss Giordi? I thought he acted—well, like a kid afraid of the teacher when he told me about you."

The black eyes, looking up at me, twinkled but she didn't smile when she answered, "I have a reputation in this town, Mr. Severson. A carefully cultivated reputation. If you had known that, perhaps you wouldn't have been so bold as to come and see me."

I couldn't help grinning. "Fools rush in."

"Exactly. Come again. My mother likes you."

"She says that Ernestine did not write the letter. She'll swear to it."

Chief Torrence closed his eyes and sighed. "Six months too soon."

"Six months . . . ?"

"I'm planning to retire at the end of the year. My wife and I have built a little place down on the Cape with heat and all, year round. Damn it, Knute, I don't need this can of worms. I don't need it at all."

I frowned. In my opinion, he'd been on the sloppy side in this whole business. No matter how I rationalized, he should have contacted Constance Giordi in the first place instead of simply taking Wharton's word for it. And as for the so-called telephone conversations with Ernestine, both the chief's and mine, how did either of us know we weren't talking to Eulalie Mayhew rather than Ernestine Wharton?

Eulalie had to be in on it. For my money. If he killed his wife, and I felt in my bones now that he had, she had to have written the letter, Constance had declared immediately that the letter was in Eulalie's hand, not Ernestine's, and she had to have pretended to be Ernestine on the phone. And now, she was coming to Wellesley, maybe was already on the way, we'd have both of them right here . . . "Are you going to dig into him on it now? Or wait for Eulalie? Better to wait, I'd say. Can't afford to flush sitting ducks and besides, we haven't got enough evidence."

I may have been wrong but I thought the chief looked brighter. I could understand to a degree, but to a very small degree. Wharton was a selectman, the chief was establishment. The publicity alone would shake the town to its foundations. But murder was murder, no matter who committed it. Torrence couldn't drag his feet much longer.

"When is she due?" he asked.

"Wharton didn't say, but my pal from L.A. called this noon. He says the house in Riverside is unoccupied as of this morning. The neighbors don't know anything about a sister, but Eulalie wasn't that chummy. Ernestine could have been there and they might not have known it. Especially since they look pretty much alike. All right, so I sound as though I'm contradicting myself, but she could have been there. I'm not closing my mind entirely. Just three-quarters. You give me a clue as to where she might have gone if she wasn't there and she isn't dead and I'll consider it."

The chief rummaged through papers, found what he was looking for. "She flew out of Boston on January tenth. To Los Angeles. If it wasn't Ernestine, it was somebody else."

"Eulalie?" I suggested.

"I suppose it could have been. She could have come on for the charade . . . God, it's hard for me to believe that the Mayhews and Wharton . . . all right, all right. She could have come on any of a number of airlines on any day previous. I wonder, did the Farleys see her? Or the Pinkhams across the street . . . no, I think they'd moved by then. It seems to me I remember the house being empty when I visited Wharton after the first letter. How about that Bird woman? If she's nutty enough to write letters?"

"Maybe she isn't so nutty."

"Maybe not. Anyway, wouldn't she have noticed Eulalie? If she were there?"

"She doesn't know Eulalie that well. And remember, how much they resemble each other. From a distance, it must be hard to tell."

"But how could he talk Eulalie into aiding and abetting? Her own sister!"

"You told me how he dated both of them, Constance Giordi says it was almost a toss-up to see which one he married. But Ernestine, the quiet one, put her foot down and grabbed him. Eulalie never married, remember. She may have had this thing about him all these years. And maybe she wasn't an accessory before the fact, only after. Like, he could have called and said, Ernestine just had an accident, she's dead and they'll blame me. You've got to come and help me cover up."

"I suppose it could be that way. It seems way out to me, but then the whole thing is . . . not only do we not know whether she's dead, we don't know how, we don't know where and we don't know what he did with the body."

I made an impatient gesture. "Okay, okay. Now we know that E. Wharton ostensibly flew to California on January 10. So whatever happened happened before that. Let's see, January 10 was a Sunday. That means on Saturday, the ninth, or even Friday, the eighth, he could have killed her. I choose the eighth because if Eulalie came out to fly back, she'd need the ninth to get here, wouldn't she? Can't we get some co-operation from the airlines on arriving L.A. passengers on January ninth?"

He wrote it down. "We can try. She needn't have used her own name."

"True. And the rosters don't always indicate whether the passenger is male or female. But let's try and get a list, anyway. We can check them all out. It will take time if we have to do that, but it may be the only way we'll get the evidence."

The chief looked shocked. "Check them all out? There'll be several hundred, I'd imagine. They don't fly dinky planes across the country."

"I know, but it's got to be done. Unless she did use Mayhew. In which case, we're in real luck. He's the devious one, she might not have thought about an alias."

"You city guys . . . you've got unlimited manpower."

"Now, Chief, you know better than that. But I'll give you a hand, as much as I can."

"Okay, okay. Then what?"

"I want to meet Eulalie. Eulalie unaware. Not professionally. Not until we have something more to go on. Socially. If she's arriving today, Brenda could give a little party, see, and naturally she'd invite Wharton and his visiting sister-in-law, it would be the neighborly thing to do."

"So what will that prove? You expect her to come right out and give herself away?"

"You never know what little mistakes people will make when they're relaxed. Wharton suspects that I suspect, I know he must. Still, he talks to me, seemingly openly. Maybe he likes to play chicken, to see how far he can go without having a head-on collision."

The chief poised his pencil. "So what else have you got now? Miss Giordi says the letter was written by Eulalie. Wharton can afford one of those handwriting experts and you know they can make black look white on the witness stand. If they're on the opposite side of the fence."

"Yes, I've seen it, seen two of them buck each other; one says yes, the other no. It may not be enough for the D.A., but I believe Constance Giordi right down the line. But we do need more and what we need can take time. Only, how much time have we got? If Eulalie takes off again, it'll mean extradition probably and you know that's often iffy. He might fly the coop, too, except that he's trapped by all his real estate. His income comes from the property and . . . but, hold it. Eulalie must have money, too. I suppose the Mayhew girls shared the estate equally?"

"As I remember. Pretty sure she knows where her next meal is coming from."

"Uhmm." Yet I still didn't think that Wharton would just abandon his considerable assets. Which explained, of course, the necessity to make people believe Ernestine was alive. As long as she was accounted for, they wouldn't wonder too much. And what was it he said, quoting Eulalie? That Ernestine, morose, had gone to Hawaii. Next stop, some foreign port? And maybe eventually a convenient demise?

The unabashed gall of the man appalled me. "We've got to get what we can as quickly as we can," I told Torrence.

Now he looked morose. "I'll put somebody on the airlines' back right away."

"How about Dennehy? And we can invite him and his girl to our little shindig. Tomorrow night, that ought to be good timing."

"But Wharton knows Dennehy, knows he's an officer."

"Sure. All the better. Wharton won't think I'm playing games. He'll figure I wouldn't be so obvious."

Chief Torrence scowled at me. "I sure hope you know what you're doing. If I get pushed off the deep end, it might even blow my pension."

"I know what I'm doing," I said confidently. Of course I did. All my instincts told me I was right. Well, what if I wasn't? No, no negative thoughts now. A little salt on the tail, and I'd catch myself a rare bird, the iron-nerved, non-blinking, quick-thinking wife killer.

The Farleys were the first to arrive at our little party. Brenda had been worried, thought they might not accept our invitation and I said, "Well, why wouldn't they? I haven't done anything to them. Not anything personal."

"I know." She looked rueful. "But you did arrest Gregg. It would be only natural for them to resent that."

"Just doing my job," I told her.

"I know." And she'd dialed their number and asked them over and Gloria had said all right. Which made Brenda feel better about the whole thing. Her doubts, expressed when I'd casually suggested a small get-together, were logical I had to admit. She knew I wasn't keen on playing host to groups and she knew I wasn't fond of Rudolph Wharton. But I sweet-talked her into it and she took the bit in her teeth with grace. If she knew my real motives, she would have hit the ceiling and I would have said, "When you're dealing with criminals, you have to think with the criminal mind." She wouldn't have gone for that either.

I went to the door when the Farleys stepped up on the

porch and let them in. "How's Gregg?" I asked immediately. No use pussyfooting.

Arlen cocked a bushy eyebrow at me. "Behaving himself." He laughed suddenly and slapped me on the back. "Sometimes I think you did us a favor. Seems as though the boy has learned his lesson."

"And I hope his parents have learned a lesson, too," said Gloria softly. She raised her voice, "He's talking about going back to school in the fall, I hope he means it. But Arlen's right, things have been better." She smiled wryly. "We actually had dinner together tonight, all four of us. And nobody argued."

I said sincerely, "I'm glad, Gloria. If I can help in any way, just yell."

She looked away and I understood. I knew something she was ashamed of, but she'd faced up to it, that's what her expression had told me. She wouldn't feel quite so easy with me for a while, but that would pass, I thought. I patted her shoulder and we moved inside.

"Who else is coming?" asked Arlen on his way to my makeshift bar in the pantry.

"Just Kevin Dennehy and Sandi Smith, he's a friend of mine on the Wellesley force and she's his girl. And Rudolph Wharton and his sister-in-law. She flew in from Los Angeles yesterday."

"Eulalie Mayhew?" asked Gloria.

"Yes."

"Well, well," said Gloria, "long time no see."

"You didn't see her in January?" I asked quickly.

"In January? Was she here in January?"

"We wouldn't know, Gloria," her husband told her. "We were in Puerto Rico in January, remember?"

"Oh, yes. I'll have my usual, Arlen, with lots of ice. How are you, Brenda? How's the baby doing?"

The doorbell rang and I excused myself, Arlen said that was all right, bartending was his real business, he did prosthetics just as a sideline; and I went to the screen door. Rudolph stood there, dressed in the best-looking sport shirt I'd seen, blue and white in a bold pattern on a kind of silky fabric and he wore white brushed denim slacks to boot, and with him was this handsome blonde. And I do mean handsome.

She was smooth, silver-gold hair, golden tan skin, pansy colored eyes and a young girl's body packaged very nicely in a beige jersey sleeveless top and sleek pants.

"Miss Mayhew, I presume," I said sounding silly, and let them in.

She put out her hand and I took it. Very soft, firm, interesting to touch. "Mr. Severson."

"Call me Knute. Good to see you, Rudolph. When did you get into Wellesley, Miss Mayhew?"

"Yesterday."

"And more important, how long are you staying?"

"That depends." She looked up at Wharton. "I'm trying to persuade Rudy to come with me, to join Ernestine in Hawaii."

"Is that so? And what does Rudolph say? Is he going?"

"I haven't convinced him as yet, but I'll keep trying." She was still looking up at him and I thought, by God, I was right. The woman's ape over him.

"Brenda!" Wharton greeted my wife enthusiastically. "Nice of you to ask us over. How lovely you look."

"Thank you, Rudy." Rudy! What an inane name.

"Do you know Gloria and Arlen Farley?" I asked Eulalie.

"I don't believe I do . . ." Politely but coolly she acknowledged the introduction.

"We met a long time ago, but you wouldn't remember." Gloria was just as cool. "You do look a great deal like Ernestine. I'd forgotten."

"Oh, I wouldn't say that." Arlen beamed. "There's a family resemblance, of course."

"What can I get you to drink?" I asked politely and while I was filling their orders, Sandi Smith arrived but without Dennehy.

"He called and told me to come over," she explained. "Something came up down at the station but he'll get here as soon as he can."

"Rudy tells me you're a detective." Eulalie made conversation while Wharton chatted with Sandi who, it seemed, had worked in his office at one time.

"That's right. On the Boston force."

"How interesting. You don't look like a detective." She slanted her pansy eyes at me.

"How is a detective supposed to look?"

"Well, for one thing, I thought you'd be wearing a gun. I thought it was standard equipment."

I gave her a quick glance. She was putting me on with that innocent look. "Not at home," I said.

"What a weird feeling it must be," Eulalie turned to Brenda, "to be married to a man who carries a gun."

Brenda bristled, but only I knew it. "He takes it off

and puts it on the bureau before he goes to bed," she said sweetly. Too sweetly.

Eulalie laughed, a tinkling laugh, as polished as her hair and face. "I'm sure it's more comfortable that way."

I walked away from them. If all the stupid conversations exchanged at cocktail parties were laid end to end . . . where the devil was Dennehy, anyway? I asked Sandi.

She moved off from the others, said cautiously, "He didn't spell it out, but he had to go pick up somebody. He said it shouldn't take him more than an hour." She checked her wristwatch. "And it's nearly an hour now since he called."

"How is Ernestine?" Gloria asked blandly.

"All right." Eulalie looked again at Wharton, added, "Physically." She moved next to him, her hands weren't touching him, but I thought they wanted to. If it was that obvious to me, it must have been equally as clear to everyone else. Including Wharton. He just stood there, drink in hand, looking superior. He did that very well.

"He made a pass at me once," said Sandi in my ear.

"What did you do?" I turned my back to the others to insure privacy.

"I quit." She smiled impishly. "He may be God's gift to women, but not to this girl."

"Wasn't that the doorbell, Knute?" Brenda, carrying a tray of hors d'oeuvres, asked me in passing.

I hadn't heard it, but when I went to the door, Dennehy was standing outside looking in.

"Hey, man." I opened the screen. "Where have you been?"

He glanced past me, shook his head. "Come on out on the porch," he suggested. I followed him and we walked around the side. We could see them through the window, talking away. Eulalie said something to Wharton and he moved out of sight with her.

"What's up?" I asked.

"We got our telephone nut."

"Hey! Who is he?"

"Well, you haven't been in on the latest. We zeroed in on that phone call Brenda got, the odd thing being where did he get the unlisted number. Which gave us some ideas of a sort and then we looked through the list again and came up with another strange one, the call from the high school principal's office, remember? It was a school day and there were people around, the office staff, teachers, kids, you know. Well, we'd questioned them before, the principal co-operated first rate, but nobody remembered anything and I'd begun to think no soap, but the second time around, after we had your phone call to put a bee in our bonnet, the school nurse remembered something that fitted. There'd been something wrong with the principal's telephone and the phone company sent a man to fix it . . ."

"That day? Why didn't the principal remember that right off the bat?"

"It just slipped his mind, I guess, didn't put the two together at all, but the nurse mentioned it because she'd come up to talk to the principal only he wasn't in his office, the telephone repair man was."

"You mean he was our boy? Of course. Pretty cute.

Nobody would think anything about a repairman, he sort of blends into the woodwork."

"That's what I thought. And he's here, there and everywhere, could have gotten your number easy, could have known about the unoccupied house, too, they'd temporarily suspended service while they were away. The chief sent me to the phone company and the phone company did some checking of their own and came up with this guy in Needham. The Needham police played their part, went to see him, found the little yellow Wellesley phone book and some very interesting literature and art, if you like pornography. Well, he cracked, told them, yeah, but so what? What harm had he done?"

"You mean he was the guy who installed our phone? I don't even remember what he looked like. No harm? What about Dolly? You've got a case of assault there."

"That's the topper, Knute. I just came back from bringing the guy in and he swears he never called the woman, never went near her. Now, you can take that with a grain of salt, who wants to confess to attacking a woman? But Dorsey buys it, at least part of it. Dorsey figures he did call her, but he says he'd bet a hundred bucks that Dolly put on that assault show all by herself. Just for attention. Dorsey says that when he went over there, she practically attacked him."

"But she was bruised. You mean, she gave herself that black eye and all?" I thought about it. "I suppose she could have thrown herself down the stairs. I didn't see a soul when I went searching and she swore I'd scared him off. The woman must be off her rocker."

Dennehy grinned. "Dorsey'll get the truth out of her.

And maybe this Craig did it after all. Dorsey's over there now, I figure, he seemed pretty eager. Like now that he knew she was crackers she interested him more. Everybody's crazy but you and me, Knute, and sometimes I wonder about you."

I tapped him lightly on the chest. "Anything from the airlines on you know who?"

"Oh, yeah. That's more big news. You guessed right, you old s.o.b. An E. Mayhew flew into Boston from L.A. on January 9. Used her real name just like you figured."

I smiled in the darkness. "Now, isn't that interesting? I'd say that gives us a basis for some pointed questions."

"Now? With all these people around? Hey, did Sandi get here?" He peered through the window. "Oh, yeah. I see her. But I don't see Wharton."

"I'll find them and bring them out on the patio. And I'll tell Sandi you'll be in shortly."

"Jeez," mused Dennehy, "I'm sure gonna feel funny about asking a selectman if he murdered his wife."

"I'll do the asking," I promised. "I've got less to lose than you if anything goes wrong."

I found Wharton and Eulalie having a tête-à-tête in the pantry and invited them out. "Something's come up," I told him in a low voice, "about your wife."

Eulalie's eyes widened but I could have announced it was raining for all the emotion Wharton showed. We went out the back door and around the house, Eulalie hanging onto his arm, joined Dennehy on the patio. The beach chairs were out and we sat in them, guests at the party. I could almost smell the tension in Eulalie. He should have picked a better actress. Dolly Selene would have carried it off.

"We have evidence," I told Wharton peremptorily, "that the so-called Ernestine letter wasn't written by your wife at all. Eulalie wrote it."

The lady made a small sound. I couldn't see her expression. Wharton said, "Who told you such a ridiculous thing? Don't you think I know my own wife's handwriting?"

"I didn't . . ." Eulalie's voice had lost its smoothness, came out in a kind of squeak.

Wharton patted her hand. "Never mind, my dear. I'll explain it. Eulalie did write the letter. At my request. Ernestine wouldn't, you see. She said as far as I was concerned, I could rot in hell."

"Did she now? You never did explain why you and your wife didn't get along. Why would she feel that strongly? She must have held a big hate."

He sighed, a long-suffering sigh. "Ernestine was unreasonably jealous. Every time I even spoke to a woman, she would accuse me of infidelity. She was even jealous of her own sister, for years her theme had been that it was Eulalie I should have married, Eulalie I wanted." Another pat, this time on the lady's shoulder. "It distressed both of us, but what could we do? Bear it patiently, hope that she would get over it."

I had to give him credit. He was telling what I termed a touching good story. "And I presume that Eulalie came here last January at your request as well."

He stiffened. Ever so slightly, but by God, I'd got to him on that one. "What do you mean, in January?"

"January ninth, to be exact. The day before your wife left on January tenth. What plane was it she came on, Dennehy?"

He recited the flight number and arrival hour.

Even in the darkness I could see Eulalie grab at Wharton's sleeve. He reached in his pocket, brought out a cigarette and lit it. The match flame lit his eyes, they were like dark marbles. "I wouldn't know about that," he said, blowing out the match.

"You wouldn't know about that? I thought you were going to explain that you called for Eulalie to come and try and change her sister's mind. But you must have remembered that what comes East has to go West again and that while E. Mayhew came only E. Wharton left."

He turned to her. "Were you here, Eulalie? You should have told me. It might have explained"—he paused—"a lot of things."

"I wasn't here." The words were bitten off. "It's a mistake. Another Mayhew."

"Isn't that a coincidence?" I asked of no one in particular. "Well, we'll just have to check that out—perhaps through the payment for the ticket, cash or check or credit card? Probably one of the latter. It was a weekend and the banks weren't open and it isn't often that a person carries two or three hundred dollars around in his or her pocket."

Wharton's cigarette gleamed brightly in the brief silence. Eulalie was breathing hard.

Wharton's cigarette made a bright arc as he took it from his mouth. "If what you say is true, it puts a different complexion on things, doesn't it?"

"It would seem to. And there's the fact that Ernestine Wharton hasn't drawn on her checking account since January, but I haven't brought that up because I'm sure you could explain that you sent her money if she needed it. I'm not sure you could prove that you did, it would be interesting to check that out."

Wharton stubbed his cigarette on the bricks. He spoke thoughtfully, "I never did understand why she left without a word. It just wasn't like her, the last word was always hers. But, if as you say, Eulalie came on, Eulalie might have the answer, mightn't she? I mean, all we have is Eulalie's word that Ernestine went to California, isn't it? And when Chief Torrence called, I suppose it is possible that Eulalie talked to him as Ernestine."

"Rudy!" Her cry was piteous.

I frowned. "You sound so bloody vague, Wharton. If Eulalie was here. Don't try and tell us you didn't know she came. And don't try and make out that you didn't send for her so that you could have proof that Ernestine left on her own two legs. They look enough alike so if anyone saw her getting into a car or taxi, say, they'd assume it was Ernestine coming out of Ernestine's house."

"That's very possible," he agreed. "But I couldn't have known any of this, couldn't have had anything to do with it, you see. Because—and this is one little fact you've overlooked in all your fine detecting—I was out of town that weekend. In Virginia. That's pretty far away, isn't it? On a Kiwanis golfer's weekend. And I can prove where I was at every moment."

I stared at him. I could have sworn he was smiling. His teeth gleamed.

"I . . ." Eulalie's ragged voice broke, she gulped, put her hand up to her mouth and jumped out. "Where's the . . . ?" she gasped.

"Upstairs," I told her quickly. I didn't blame her for being sick. He was throwing her to the wolves and she knew it now. How long had he been stringing her along, "Just wait, Eulalie, when the hue and cry is over we'll be together . . ." She must have gotten impatient and the Wellesley phone calls, especially mine, must have made her nervous. How the hell was I to guess Patsy Oliver was a man? But it didn't matter, it had brought her back. A boomerang for our side.

The back door slammed after her and I told Wharton, "It doesn't matter whether you were here or not. You could have done the job, left for an alibi and brought Eulalie here to clean up the loose ends. Or"—I had another thought—"maybe she didn't know Ernestine was dead? Maybe you conned her into thinking that Ernestine had really left you and you'd be blamed, that she'd have to cover up for you in some way. You're an expert in bringing Eulalie to heel, although how you kept her dangling for twenty years is more than I can figure. And I don't think I'd care to know the knack. But, yes, it could have been that way. It kind of bothered me to think that she'd take part in her own sister's killing. Or, did you just make out it was an accident? If so, where's the body?"

"You're accusing me of murder?" Wharton's tone was icy. "Hadn't you better advise me of my rights?"

And I opened my mouth to do so, but at that moment someone came rapidly around the back of the house, someone running stopped and while I was turning to see who it was, turning in alarm because there had been a sound to the running that made my hackles rise, there was a flash and I knew what it was even as my ears rang from the shot; I instinctively dove for the brick floor. Lying there, I heard shouts and somebody screaming.

I got up, slowly, Dennehy, too; and saw Wharton lying crumpled in a heap. Standing on the porch was a clump of people, frozen into position, and standing six feet away from me was Eulalie, sobbing.

She'd gone upstairs, taken my gun off the bureau, come down and killed him. Just like that. And he hadn't told us where his wife's body was. And Eulalie swore and swore again that she didn't know, didn't know, didn't know!

It was the day before the christening that Mercy Bird came over to tell us she'd figured it out.

She made her announcement in her usual abrupt manner and Brenda, who was still on the edgy side, couldn't bear to look across at Wharton's empty house, wouldn't even glance at a line about Eulalie in the papers, stared at Mercy aghast. "You mean, you know where he buried her?" she managed to ask. "But how could you possibly . . . ?"

Mercy, clad this day in a brown wool outfit even though the thermometer read 82 degrees, nodded emphatically and produced a pad of paper covered with scrawling notes. "Now, Ernestine was murdered prior to January eight, that's when Rudolph flew off to Virginia."

I nodded.

"And Eulalie swears that she didn't know her sister was dead, that she never saw the body."

"Right. And ridiculous as it seems, I halfway believe her. Whether the jury will is another question. She's got E. Leo Barley to defend her."

"Well, I believe her and I'll tell you why. I think Ernestine told Wharton she was through, she'd get a divorce, change the financial set-up, leave him like she found him, a nobody from nowhere, and he picked up something and let her have it. That I guess we won't know until we find the body, just how he killed her. Anyway, then he called Eulalie and pulled the strings on the puppet. So that, in all probability, Ernestine was disposed of on January sixth or seventh."

I thought about what she'd said. "It had to be the seventh. Gregg Farley talked to her early that week, he thinks it was on a Wednesday, which was the sixth, because he had a half day off from school on Wednesday."

Mercy looked triumphant. "Then that proves it!"

"Proves what?" asked Brenda, interested in spite of herself.

"The Pinkhams moved the first of the year. They had contracted for their new porch, the better to sell the house, but it hadn't been done, frozen ground, you see, and the workmen came after they'd gone because we had an early January thaw. They dug the foundation on Wednesday and Thursday and they poured the cement on a Friday morning, that would be January eighth, I know because I had the flu and I was in bed and had nothing better to do than watch them dig and pour. All of which means that Rudolph Wharton could have carried his wife's body across the street during the night of January seventh, put it in the hole, covered it with dirt or stones, they had piles of stones for fill, and she was totally entombed on January eighth. Knute, Ernestine's body is under your front porch!"

Brenda burst into tears. "Knute," she wailed, "how could you?" and rushed into the house.

"Under the porch?" I asked Mercy weakly, and then, hearing sounds from the house, "What did I do?"

Mercy looked at me owlishly. "You moved her out of the big wicked city and brought her to the country where it's quiet and peaceful."